THE GUNSMITH

396

A DIFFERENT TRADE

J. R. ROBERTS

JOVE BOOKS, NEW YORK

THE BERKLEY PUBLISHING GROUP
Published by the Penguin Group
Penguin Group (USA) LLC
375 Hudson Street, New York, New York 10014

USA • Canada • UK • Ireland • Australia • New Zealand • India • South Africa • China

penguin.com

A Penguin Random House Company

A DIFFERENT TRADE

A Jove Book / published by arrangement with the author

For information, address: The Berkley Publishing Group,
a division of Penguin Group (USA) LLC,
375 Hudson Street, New York, New York 10014.

ISBN: 978-0-515-15499-3

PUBLISHING HISTORY
Jove mass-market edition / December 2014

PRINTED IN THE UNITED STATES OF AMERICA

10 9 8 7 6 5 4 3 2 1

Cover illustration by Sergio Giovine.

Mess with the Bull and You Get the Horns

While he was crouched down low, Clint drove a few quick punches into Westin's midsection. The big man's stomach felt more like a slab of beef wrapped around a post. Clint was still doing his best to chop that post down when a pair of beefy forearms dropped onto his shoulder like a sledgehammer. The impact stole some of the breath from Clint's lungs and dropped him to one knee.

Leering down at him, Westin hunched over a bit as he asked, "Did that hurt?"

Clint's reply to the taunt was to reach up with one hand, take a firm grip on Westin's beard, and pull him down sharply. The big man's chin thumped against the edge of the bar, and he staggered back while letting out a pained roar. Clint pulled himself to his feet and put every bit of strength he could muster behind a right cross to the head.

Although Westin was hurt by the last blow, he had enough of his wits about him to catch Clint's incoming punch. The sound of knuckles slapping against his left palm still hung in the air when Westin tightened his grip around Clint's fist. "You made a whole lot of mistakes here, boy," he snarled into Clint's face.

When Clint tried to pull his hand free, he only felt Westin's grip become even tighter. Already, sharp jolts of pain shot up through his arm.

"You picked the wrong saloon to come into," Westin said. "You opened your mouth when you should'a kept it shut. And you raised a hand to a man who can put you six feet under anytime he chooses."

Clint balled up his other fist and took a swing at Westin. That punch bounced off the big man's side, and before Clint could follow up, the bones in his trapped hand were mercilessly ground together. Even though Clint was able to stand up in front of the bigger man, he couldn't do much else at that moment.

ONE

Larga Noche, New Mexico

Most towns had a story that could be read in the way they were laid out, where they were located, or what sorts of business were run within its boundaries. Some towns had played host to well-known events or even legendary ones. Others simply . . . were. As far as Clint could tell, Larga Noche was one of the latter.

Located close enough to the desert for the winds to carry a harsh warmth along with the gritty texture of sunbaked sand, it wasn't trapped within the scorched rocks like so many other settlements. There was a meandering stream on the town's northern edge and some vistas to the southwest that were downright breathtaking when the sun hit them in the morning. None of these things was reason enough for a town to be built, however. There were no major trade routes passing through. The closest railroad station was a day and a half's ride away. Even getting there by stagecoach required a five-mile ride to meet a driver who only bothered to come along every other week. Clint didn't need to know why every town had come to be, but he usually could get a sense for such a thing after spending a minimal amount of time there. Larga Noche might as well have sprung up from the arid dirt like an old tortoise that didn't have the good sense to draw its head straight back into its shell again.

As far as he could tell, there was barely any organization to the town at all. Its crooked streets were irregularly spaced. Some buildings looked to have burned down years ago and been left to rot while others were immaculately maintained by their owners. But beyond any of that or anything else that could be seen or heard, Clint simply felt as if Larga Noche wasn't going to be there for very long. It was similar to crossing a bridge that creaked and moaned with every step. A man in that spot didn't need to know why the bridge had been built or how long it had been there. He simply knew he had to finish his walk to the other side before that shoddy structure inevitably fell apart.

Scowling at the town as he rode through it, Clint patted the neck of his Darley Arabian stallion, Eclipse. "I know you're thirsty, boy. We'll get you something to drink and put a roof over your head for the night. Hopefully we won't be here much longer than that."

When he looked up again, Clint saw a couple who looked to be somewhere in their late fifties. Judging by the near-lifeless stares they wore, neither the old man nor his wife was surprised to hear such words coming from a stranger. In fact, they seemed just as ready as Clint to get the hell out of that place. Even though it didn't look like he'd hurt any feelings, Clint tipped his hat to them and smiled in a casual apology. The old man grunted under his breath and pulled the woman across the street toward a store with shoes displayed in its front window.

"Might warn me next time," Clint grumbled to Eclipse.

"We've got business to conduct here, and the better it goes, the faster we can leave."

Clint continued riding down a street that had been called Linden at the south end of town and, for some unknown reason, changed into Preston Avenue farther north. Before long, he spotted a street that branched off to the right. If not for the ruckus coming from that direction, Clint might have overlooked the street altogether. As it was, a man would have had to be blind and deaf to move past it without noticing the cloud of dust being kicked up less than sixty yards away.

Normally, hearing a whinnying horse wasn't enough to catch Clint's undivided attention. Since there wasn't much else to look at apart from a shoddy town, he was all too eager to investigate what had made the animal so unhappy. It didn't take him long to spot the woman dressed in dirty jeans and a dusty flannel shirt trying to grab hold of the anxious horse's reins. When the horse turned its eyes toward her, it reared up and started churning its front hooves in the air. The woman in the dusty clothes was smart and fast enough to dive to one side before those angry hooves came down again.

"Easy, girl!" the woman said as soon as she hit the ground. "Just let me—"

Before the woman could finish what she'd been saying, the angry horse pounded its hooves against the dirt and then turned away from her while shaking its head as though a bee were trapped in its ear. Clint didn't like the erratic way the horse was bucking and kicking, so he snapped his reins to get his own stallion moving a bit faster. He arrived just in time to lean over and scoop the woman up in one arm before the angry horse's rear legs snapped back in a powerful kick.

The woman was much prettier up close, even when she pinched her features into an expression of angry surprise. "Let go of me," she said. She had the strength to back up her request and nearly wriggled loose from Clint's grasp. When he tightened his arm around her waist, Clint was pulled from his saddle and barely managed to break his fall before breaking his neck.

"What the hell is wrong with you?" Clint snapped as he rolled on top of her. "I'm trying to . . . look out!"

The angry horse's rump was so close to Clint and the woman that it blocked the sunlight from their eyes. Wrapping both arms around the woman, Clint rolled away from a water trough as the horse's rear legs lashed out to smash through the long wooden container. Wooden planks cracked and broke into splinters. Water sprayed in every direction and ran onto the ground. When he felt the impact of those hooves thumping against the ground again, Clint was just as nervous as he'd been when shots were fired at him.

If either one of them caught even a glancing blow from those raging kicks, Clint or the woman would be pulverized. He wrapped his arms around her even tighter, covered her with his body, and waited for the longest couple of seconds he'd suffered through in a long while. After those seconds had passed, Clint twisted his head around to get a look at the wild horse. He let out the breath he'd been holding once he saw the animal point its nose away from them and start running down the street.

"Stay here," he said to the woman. "I'll be right back."

"Where are you going?" she asked.

"To fetch that horse before it kicks someone's head off their shoulders!"

TWO

Clint swung up into his saddle and snapped his reins within the space of a few heartbeats. In that short span of time, the wild horse had continued farther down the street to scatter several small groups of folks who'd been watching the commotion from what had once been a safe distance. Fortunately for them, they were all able to dive through a doorway or duck into an alley before being trampled by the rampaging animal.

Now that there was some distance between him and the other horse, Clint could pick a side from which to approach without being knocked into next week. Keeping one hand on his reins, he reached down with his other hand to snatch the length of rope hanging from the side of his saddle. By the time he got a lasso spinning, the horse had set its sights on a tall man and two children. Both young ones were pressed against the side of a clothier, boxed in between an outhouse and a stack of crates positioned next to the shop's side entrance. With nowhere else to go in the short time that remained, the tall man spread his arms and stood in front of the children to shield them from what was charging straight at them.

Although this wasn't the first time Clint had held a rope in his hand, he wasn't about to gamble anyone's life on his skill with it unless there was no other choice. Quickly gripping his reins between his teeth, he used that hand to draw the modified Colt from his holster and fire a shot into the air well above the runaway horse's head. Hearing the explosive sound, the wild horse reared up once again.

Now that the horse had stopped and was even stretching its neck while lifting its head to the sky, Clint was given the best target he could hope for. He quickly got the lasso spinning again, raised it high, and sent it flying toward the other horse as he rode by. The lasso dropped around the wild horse's neck and Clint cinched it tight with a few sharp tugs. After wrapping his end of the rope around his saddle horn, he rode down the street toward the edge of town.

Although Clint had his sights set on the wide-open terrain beyond Larga Noche's eastern border, he didn't have to ride that far before the horse he'd roped began to slow its pace. As soon as he heard a few tired breaths come from the horse's mouth, Clint turned around to smirk at the pretty young woman who'd almost been trampled, and he tipped his hat. Naturally, that was the moment when the horse within Clint's noose caught its second wind.

Without a hint of warning, the horse lurched forward sharply enough to loosen the other end of the rope from Clint's saddle horn. As soon as it had enough slack, it broke into a gallop. Clint was lucky to hang on to his rope, but his luck ran out when he was yanked clean from his saddle. One moment he was trying to get a better look at the horse's pretty owner and the next, he was about to land belly-first onto the ground. Clint reflexively twisted around before he hit, somehow managing to land on one side and a leg. The impact hurt like hell, but no bones were busted in the process.

Perhaps inspired by the sight of open ground not too far ahead of its nose, the horse moved toward the edge of town with Clint skidding behind it. Buildings, wagons, and barrels rushed past Clint on both sides. Before long, he knew he wouldn't see much of anything unless he let go of that rope. Stubbornness won out over common sense when Clint tightened his grip rather than let go after hanging on for this long. He was getting ready to swallow his pride when the horse slowed to a walk while breathing in heavy, tired gulps. Even at that less vigorous pace, Clint's boots were still creating a pair of shallow ruts as he was dragged down the street.

To his left was a hitching post in front of a short row of storefronts, so he maneuvered himself in that direction. Once there, he braced a foot against the post and pulled back on the rope. Despite the extra leverage he'd gained, Clint was still convinced he would be forced to let the horse go before being dragged all the way into the next town. At that moment, however, the horse lost its last bit of steam and gave up on its attempt to flee. Its head hung low as it gave a few parting tugs on Clint's rope in a final show of defiance.

Removing his foot from the side of the post, Clint walked toward the horse while reeling in the rope. "It's all right, folks," he said to the scattered locals, who were already losing interest in the show. "I've got this under control."

The people who were still watching him were now even less interested than they'd been a moment ago. The only exception to that was the man who'd been protecting the two children when the horse had reared. He ran up to Clint and slapped him on the shoulder. "Thanks, mister!" he said. "Thought we were gonna be put through that wall back there."

"I should be able to keep that from happening but you

might want to tend to those two before things get out of hand again."

The grateful man was about to say something else when he glanced back at the spot where he'd left the two children. Rather than staying put, the two young ones were already wandering into the street to get a closer look at the animal that had almost done them in. "Aw, fer Christ's sake," the man said. "The both of you won't be happy until you get your necks broke! Then your ma would skin me alive!"

With that, the man hurried to gather the children in such a rush that the winded horse being led by Clint almost worked itself into a lather again. It was calmed by a hand that reached out to gently rub the horse's head close to its ear.

"You've got a real knack with horses," the pretty young woman said.

Clint looked over at her and realized she was even more attractive when she was calm than when they'd been wrangling the out-of-control horse. She had a thick, dark brown hair that was tied back behind her head to show high cheekbones, dark blue eyes, and a wide, full mouth. "Either that," she added, "or you're just a fool with a lucky streak."

"Well, thank you," Clint replied. "I think."

"Whichever it is, I'm mighty grateful for your help. Anything I might be able to do to repay you?"

He smiled at her. "I can think of a few things."

THREE

As much as Clint would have liked to continue his conversation with the horse's pretty owner, there was still business to conduct. It made it even easier for him to get back to that business when he decided that wrapping it up would allow him to get back to other matters that much quicker. Before parting ways with her, Clint got three key pieces of information.

First of all, he asked the lady for her name. It was Danielle Hagerty.

Second, he set up a time and place where they could meet again.

Third, he needed directions to the Dig Dog Saloon.

Danielle had furrowed her brow when he'd asked her about that last one. "The Digger?" she'd asked. "Why would you want to go there?"

"Is that another name for the Dig Dog?" Clint asked.

"One name's as ridiculous as the other."

"Good point. How do I get there?"

"Why do you want to go there?" she asked as though Clint had wanted directions to the middle of a swamp.

Instead of explaining every reason he had for being in Larga Noche, Clint simply told her, "I'm meeting a friend. Shouldn't keep me occupied for too long, so it won't interfere with our own meeting."

She showed him a mischievous smirk and said, "I don't know why I let you talk me into this."

"Into what?" Clint replied. "It's just a meal and—"

"Right," she cut in. "It's the *and* part that's got me concerned."

"Concerned or anxious?"

Danielle allowed that to hang in the air between them before grabbing the horse's reins, turning on her heel, and walking back to the stable where Clint had originally found her. He looked around, spotted Eclipse calmly waiting for him a short distance away, and went to retrieve him.

When Clint got to the stable, the horse that had bolted not too long ago now stood in a stall of its own and was quietly working on a feed bag. He allowed Eclipse to drink from the water trough out in front.

After the stallion had drunk his fill, Clint mounted up and called out to Danielle, "I'll be back before you know it." In response, she pretended as though she'd already forgotten he was there.

Even as he thought back to it a short while later, he had to smile at her display. Mostly, he was looking forward to seeing that face again no matter what expression it wore. Unfortunately, Clint had more time than expected to think back to his conversation with Danielle as he wandered the streets looking for Sharp Bend.

When she'd given him directions to the saloon, Danielle did indeed tell him to look for Sharp Bend off Third Avenue. At the time, however, he'd thought she meant to just look for a sharp bend in Third Avenue. After it branched off Linden

Street, Third Avenue was full of sharp bends and Clint figured it would be quicker to just investigate every one.

He couldn't have been more wrong.

Before Clint reached the end of one sharp bend, he found another. And when he reached the end of that one, he nearly forgot how far back he needed to go to return to where he'd started. There wasn't much to see along those sharp bends. Mostly, they were just lined with a few shops, homes, or the occasional saloon. Naturally, none of those saloons was the one he was looking for. Clint was just about to give up the wild-goose chase when he noticed a sign nailed to a post at yet another small street branching off Third. The sign read, SHARP BEND. So her reference was for a street named Sharp Bend, not a bend in a road that was sharp. To top things off, as Clint rode down that street, the only bend he came to wasn't even particularly sharp.

"I'm really beginning to hate this town," he grumbled.

After rounding that single gentle bend, Clint found himself in the closest thing to a saloon district he'd found in Larga Noche. The Dig Dog Saloon was on his left a short ways up the street. A bit farther along and next to that saloon was a taller, narrower building with a colorful sign hanging in front of it. Clint couldn't make out the lettering on that sign just yet, but it was impossible to miss the tiger drawn onto it. Across from that establishment was a place with two floors and windows decorated in expensive curtains. The softer colors and number of women lounging in front of that place made it clear that its primary specialty wasn't liquor or gambling. Even from a distance, Clint had caught the attention of a couple of those ladies so he tipped his hat to them and moved along.

Of the three places, the Dig Dog wasn't the one that Clint would have chosen if he was just looking for somewhere to slake his thirst. When he saw the crudely drawn picture on the front window, that opinion only grew stronger. Stepping in through the batwing doors, Clint was already making plans to visit the other two places down the street.

The Dig Dog resembled any number of saloons Clint had visited across the country. There was a long bar on one side of the main room, a small stage on the other, and several tables scattered in between. The woman on the stage was attractive, if a bit past her prime, but she merely sat on a stool beside a bearded fellow plucking a lazy tune on a guitar. Only two of the tables were occupied by card players, who looked to have been there since before the place was built. The only thing that stood out in Clint's eyes was the bar itself. Part of that was due to the impressive array of bottles on the shelves behind it. The other part was the fact that the barkeep had just been grabbed by the man he'd been talking to and pulled halfway over the polished wooden surface.

FOUR

Clint made his way over to the bar and stood close enough to the other two men to hear what they were saying, but far enough away from them to be out of swinging distance.

"Are you deaf?" the man on Clint's side of the bar growled. He was a tall fellow with a muscular build that tested the strength of the stitching on his dusty cotton shirt. Thick brown hair hung down past his shoulders and was tied back with a leather cord in a sloppy manner that barely served to keep his face from being covered. That face was cruel, marred by scars, and partially covered by a thick, brushy beard.

The barkeep looked to be somewhere in his early forties. Although his arms were spindly and his chest was narrow, a rounded belly could be seen now that he'd been lifted up by the man in front of him. Although his straw-like red hair had been trimmed to a respectable length, it sprouted at unruly angles from his scalp. "I'm not deaf," he said. "I heard you. It's just that—"

"Just that what?" the other man snapped as he pulled the barkeep a few inches closer to him.

Since he hadn't seemed to have been noticed just yet, Clint leaned back against the bar and loudly cleared his throat.

Both of the other two men at the bar turned to look at him. The big one with the long hair looked ready to bite Clint's head off and spit it through the window. The barkeep, on the other hand, smiled warmly and asked, "Can I get you something?"

"Actually, yes," Clint replied. "I'll take a beer."

Since the barkeep couldn't move, he shifted his eyes over to look at the man that was holding him on top of the bar.

The man next to Clint easily outweighed him by fifty pounds. When he glared over at him, the bearded man's eye twitched as if it were trying to leap from its socket. "What the hell's wrong with you, mister?"

Clint shrugged. "I'm thirsty."

When the big man smiled, it looked more like an animal baring its teeth. "Why don't you just hop on over the bar and help yourself. Me and this pregnant pencil here have just a bit more talking to do."

"Why don't you let the man go so he can do his job?" Clint asked.

That captured a bit more of the big man's attention. Before he could say anything, the barkeep quickly sputtered, "There's no need for more unpleasantness. Especially not to my customers."

"I'll be unpleasant to anyone I damn well please," the big man said.

"I need every customer I can get, Westin," the barkeep said. "Without them, I won't be able to pay you anything."

"You ain't been paying me now. That's the goddamn problem."

Clint looked about at the rest of the people in that saloon. Despite a few cautious glances tossed toward the bar, the gamblers kept playing, the guitar player kept strumming, and the drinkers kept drinking. The only one to move a muscle was the girl onstage, who'd gotten up from her stool to walk behind the piano.

Placing both hands upon the bar, Clint hopped up onto it and swung both legs over to come down on the other side. "Can I get anything for you?" he asked.

It took a moment, but Westin soon realized the question had been directed at him. "Give me a whiskey from one of them real pretty bottles on the top shelf."

Clint looked down near the bartender's feet. "There's some fancy bottles of something down here. How much for a sip of that?"

"Th-That's—"

Westin interrupted the barkeep's stuttering with a violent shake that caused the redhead's flailing legs to knock into some glasses behind him. "Them's are no charge," the big man said. "See, Leo? That's how you win over new customers."

"You're Leo?" Clint asked.

The barkeep nodded.

"Leo Parker?"

"I am."

"Well, that changes things."

"I'm sick of you already," Westin grunted. "Get the hell out of my sight before I mess you up even worse than I intend on messing up this here barkeep!"

Clint shook his head. "I'm not going anywhere. You are."

"Really?" Westin said through another ugly smile. "And what if I don't?"

"Put me to the test and see for yourself."

FIVE

Like most big men, Westin thought his size alone was enough to win any fight for him. He kept hold of Leo's neck in one hand while straightening up to his full height and nodding as though nobody could have guessed how massive he truly was. "You sure you want to go there, boy?"

And like any man who had any self-respect, Clint felt an urge to throw a punch when someone called him "boy." Since Westin obviously knew that, Clint wasn't about to play into his hands. "Let the barkeep go," he said, "and walk out."

"That what you want?"

Clint nodded once.

Although Westin let go of Leo's shirt, it wasn't until after he'd slammed the redhead's face against the top of the bar with just enough force to bloody his nose. He then took one step away from the bar and planted his feet. "If'n you want me to leave, you'll have to make me."

"How did I know you were going to say that?"

"Because maybe you got a brain in your head. Gotta be smarter than this one anyway," Westin said while giving Leo a quick backhanded swat.

Clint was already stooping a bit to reach for the fancy bottles kept under the bar and out of plain sight. When he stood up, he was holding something other than overpriced whiskey in his hands. Gripping the sawed-off shotgun that had been kept at the barkeep's knee level, Clint thumbed back both hammers and held the weapon at the ready. "Now you've got two choices," Clint said. "Walk out or be carried out of here after being scraped off the walls, ceiling, and floor."

"You think this is the first time I seen that scattergun?" Westin asked. "If I'm supposed to quake in my boots at the sight of it, I gotta think you have the sand to pull them triggers."

For a few moments, both men stared at each other. The rest of the saloon had grown quiet, and once again, the woman on the stage was the only one moving. While the other customers kept their heads down and prayed not to be noticed, she stepped out from behind the piano to show Clint that she was now carrying a pistol that had most likely been stashed back there.

"I can usually sniff out a lawman," Westin said as he took one step toward Clint, "and you don't strike me as anyone with a badge pinned to him somewhere. That means you're most likely someone trying to do the right thing by helping this little runt here. Trust me, the barkeep brought this on himself."

"I would have been glad to let the two of you conduct your business," Clint told him. "But I've got business of my own with that man."

"That a fact?"

"Yes, sir. And I won't have it ruined by the likes of you."

"That's just too bad, then." Without another word, Westin lunged forward to slap the barrel of the shotgun aside with a thick paw of a hand.

The move came much quicker than Clint had anticipated

and would have been enough to send any shot fired from the shortened barrels into one of the nearby walls. Instead of pulling his triggers, however, Clint snapped the other end of the shotgun around to crack it against the side of Westin's head. As the bigger man reeled back from the blow, Clint hopped over the bar to stand toe to toe with him.

As Westin reeled from taking the knock to the head, Clint opened the shotgun and dumped both shells onto the floor. The ammunition was still rattling against the boards near their feet when Westin plucked the shotgun from Clint's grasp and swung it viciously at his jaw. If Clint hadn't been quick enough to duck beneath the attack, it could very well have put him out of the fight altogether.

While he was crouched down low, Clint drove a few quick punches into Westin's midsection. The big man's stomach felt more like a slab of beef wrapped around a post. Clint was still doing his best to chop that post down when a pair of beefy forearms dropped onto his shoulder like a sledgehammer. The impact stole some of the breath from Clint's lungs and dropped him to one knee.

Leering down at him, Westin hunched over a bit as he asked, "Did that hurt?"

Clint's reply to the taunt was to reach up with one hand, take a firm grip on Westin's beard, and pull him down sharply. The big man's chin thumped against the edge of the bar, and he staggered back while letting out a pained roar. Clint pulled himself to his feet and put every bit of strength he could muster behind a right cross to the head.

Although Westin was hurt by the last blow, he had enough of his wits about him to catch Clint's incoming punch. The sound of knuckles slapping against his left palm still hung in the air when Westin tightened his grip around Clint's fist. "You made a whole lot of mistakes here, boy," he snarled into Clint's face.

When Clint tried to pull his hand free, he only felt Westin's grip become even tighter. Already, sharp jolts of pain shot up through his arm.

"You picked the wrong saloon to come into," Westin said. "You opened your mouth when you should'a kept it shut. And you raised a hand to a man who can put you six feet under anytime he chooses."

Clint balled up his other fist and took a swing at Westin. That punch bounced off the big man's side, and before Clint could follow up, the bones in his trapped hand were mercilessly ground together. Even though Clint was able to stand up in front of the bigger man, he couldn't do much else at that moment.

"Look at the idiot you stuck your neck out for," Westin said. "He don't even have enough of a brain to know when he should run. It ain't like he'll get many more chances after this little dance."

Sure enough, Leo had his back to the wall of shelves behind the bar as though he were stuck there by half a barrel of glue.

"I'll only say this one more time," Clint said. "Leave now."

"And I'll say this one more time: Or what?"

"Or I draw the pistol that I've left in its holster this long just to keep this from getting too messy."

Westin's eyes darted downward to verify Clint's claim. The Colt wasn't easy to miss, and though he wasn't shocked to see it there, Westin let go of Clint's hand. "That brings us right back around to where we started."

"You mean about whether or not I've got the sand to pull a trigger?" Clint asked. "Can you look in my eyes and have any doubt of that?"

Westin took a look for himself, and before he could respond to what he saw, someone spoke up from a few paces behind him.

"You shouldn't doubt me on that count," the woman who'd been on the stage not too long ago said. She held her pistol in a two-handed grip and stared at Westin over the top of its barrel. When he positioned himself so he could shift his gaze between her and Clint, Westin said, "I should've guessed you'd need the help of a woman, boy."

"Just get the hell out of my sight," Clint replied.

Westin casually turned to look at Leo, who was still glued to the wall behind the bar. "You remember what I told you before we was interrupted?"

"Yes," Leo replied.

"Then I'm done here." Westin turned his back on all the guns in the room as if none of them were capable of making him bleed, and he walked out through the front door.

Once he was certain the big man wasn't about to come back, Clint looked over at the woman and asked, "What took you so damn long?"

SIX

It wasn't until after he'd drunk the beer he'd been given that Clint actually took a good look at the woman who'd been on the stage when he'd first arrived. Before then, either she was on the opposite side of the room, or he was more interested in the gun she'd been carrying. Now that the storm had passed and she was right in front of him, he could see that she was much younger than he'd originally thought.

"I'm so sorry," she said.

"For what?" Clint asked.

"For taking so long to get to you. I guess I was just a bit scared."

Clint set his beer down and said, "I was just riled up when I asked you that. You came in at just the right time. That big ape needed to be knocked around a bit before he would go quietly. Any sooner and he would've had enough wind in his sails to make things a whole lot worse."

She smiled and nodded before extending a slender hand. "I'm Madeline."

When Clint shook her hand, he found out that she was

even softer than she looked. “Clint Adams. Pleasure to meet you.”

Madeline’s skin was pale and smooth. Her straight black hair fell down to well past her shoulders and was held back with a dark red ribbon. Up close, Clint could also see that the luscious red color of her lips wasn’t there because of any paint or cream.

“Excuse me,” said a voice from over Clint’s shoulder, “but do I know you?”

Clint turned to find the barkeep at his post, studying him with nervous eyes. “I just got to town,” Clint replied.

“Yes, but it seemed like you knew me. You know . . . before when you asked if I was Leo Parker. Well . . . I am.”

The sweet scent of Madeline’s hair had filled Clint’s nose as she’d leaned in to give him a grateful kiss on the cheek. He was somewhat distracted until she turned around and walked back to the stage, where the guitar player was already starting in on another song. He had to keep from watching the sway of Madeline’s hips before getting distracted all over again. “Right. We don’t know each other, but we do have a mutual acquaintance. A man from California by the name of Gregor Petrovich.”

Leo’s eyes widened and he smiled broadly. “Ah yes! Gregor! Where is he?”

“That’s just it. He couldn’t make it on account of a boat coming in from South America that he needs to meet personally. It got held up in a storm, but he wanted to make sure you got your delivery. Gregor’s a friend and I was headed this direction anyway so I brought the shipment on his behalf.”

Gregor Petrovich was more of a friendly business associate than a friend. A hustler in the import and export trade, Gregor was the sort of man who was quick to buy someone a drink and offer them a way to make a few quick dollars.

He was also the type to get himself into trouble after playing too many angles at once. Rather than owe a man like that a favor, Clint decided to square their account by taking a small package to Larga Noche.

Obviously not interested on any of that, Leo asked, "Where is it?"

"With my horse."

"You left it with your horse?"

"Isn't that what I just said?"

Leo blinked and twitched as if he'd just been struck by lightning. Finally, he managed to ask, "Can you get it for me?"

"Sure," Clint replied. "That's why I'm here." He tipped back his beer mug and then set it down. "Have that filled when I get back."

"Of course!"

Clint stepped outside, rummaged through his saddlebags, and retrieved a package that was wrapped in paper and tied up in twine. He tucked it under his arm and headed back into the saloon. A few strides short of the bar, Clint showed the package to Leo and then tossed it in a high, slow arc. "There you go."

The barkeep stretched out both hands and gasped to catch the package like it was a swaddled baby. "Be careful!"

"I was. Those things are wrapped up tight enough to survive a tumble down a steep slope."

Just when it seemed Leo couldn't look more panicked, he did. "Did you drop this down a slope?"

As much as Clint wanted to say that he had, just to see how many more veins would stand out on Leo's forehead, he took the higher road. "Of course I didn't. I cared for that whatever-it-is like it was my firstborn."

"Good. After what I paid for it, that's the least I'd expect."

Everyone in the saloon had gone back to what they'd been

doing before Westin's departure. Clint stood and watched as the barkeep lovingly tugged at the twine so he could unwrap his package. Before he could reveal what was inside, however, he turned his back to the rest of the room and huddled over it in privacy.

"What is it?" Clint asked.

"Hmm?"

"The package. What's inside?"

At first, Leo didn't seem ready to show what he was hiding. He then turned partway around and quickly put his back to Clint once again as he said, "You can find out when everyone else does."

"When's that?" Clint asked.

"In a day or two. Perhaps next week."

Clint let out a long sigh. "After I rode all the way from California with that thing, you won't even let me get a look?"

"Curious, Mr. Adams?"

"Yes!"

Clearly enjoying the anticipation he was building, Leo kept the package hidden from sight as he said, "I don't know. Once word gets out about this, things will be plenty different around here."

Now Clint was even more curious. The fact that he was playing directly into Leo's little display only made it worse. Finally, he said, "Just show me what it is before I find that Westin fellow and invite him to finish what he started."

Leo didn't look as though he believed Clint's threat, but he could tell his audience's patience was wearing thin. Grudgingly, he stepped aside and gestured toward the three bottles of clear liquid that were standing amid the mess of snapped twine and ripped paper. "All right," he said. "Take a look for yourself. Just don't tell anyone else about it until I'm ready to do it up right."

Clint leaned forward and squinted at the bottles. "What else is there?"

"Nothing. That's it."

"That's the precious merchandise I rode all the way out here to deliver in person?"

Leo nodded. "I paid extra for it to be shipped with the most care possible."

"Just a couple of bottles?"

"Three. That's a few, not a couple."

"I can't even read what's on the labels."

"Give me a moment," Leo said as he flipped through a few pieces of paper that had been wedged in between two bottles.

Clint tossed a halfhearted wave and started walking toward the front door. "Forget it."

"Where are you going?"

"I need to put my horse up for the night."

"And that's more interesting than this?" Leo asked.

"Oh God, yes."

SEVEN

When Clint led Eclipse back to the first stable in town he'd seen, Danielle walked outside to greet him. Her sleeves were rolled up and she peeled off a pair of gloves that were covered in loose hay. She gave him a wide smile and placed one hand on her hip while waiting for him to come to a stop.

"That's a handsome boy," she said.

"Why, thank you," Clint replied. "You're not so bad yourself."

"I meant the horse. What's his name?"

"Eclipse."

Danielle reached out to pat the Darley Arabian's nose, which was received very well. "I think he likes me."

"That's why we came all the way back here for a stall."

"Is it?" she asked while glancing over to Clint.

"Actually," he said while hooking a thumb toward Eclipse, "that's why he wanted to come back. I had other ideas."

"Did you, now? How about we start with the stall? Follow me."

Clint was more than happy to follow her since that meant

getting a nice, lingering look at Danielle's backside wrapped in muddy denim. Her brown hair was unruly after the hard work she'd been doing, which did nothing to take away from her appeal. In fact, the sweaty shirt and dirty jeans clung to her rounded curves in a stunning way.

The stable was a fairly good size. One wide path led from the front to the back of the barn-sized structure, which had three horse stalls on either side. The stall in the back corner was occupied by the horse that had broken loose earlier that day. Now it was calmly chewing on half an apple.

"Let's put Eclipse right here," Danielle said as she pushed open the gate to the first stall. Thc Darley Arabian followed her in and immediately found a trough of water against the back wall. "As for you," she said to Clint, "I think you should go right here."

Clint found himself being pushed against the nearest post. As soon as his shoulders bumped against the wooden support, Danielle was pressed against him. "What's this now?"

Reaching up to slide both hands around the back of his head, she whispered, "Can't you tell?"

Clint may have been taken slightly off guard, but he wasn't about to push her away. He placed his hands upon her hips and savored the feel of her nicely rounded curves. "I was expecting to have to go through a little sweet talk before I got this close to you."

She shook her head. Since she was less than an inch away from him, her lips brushed against Clint's mouth as she told him, "I don't like that sort of nonsense. I saw something I wanted and now I'm taking it." As she spoke, Danielle eased one hand between Clint's legs.

Moving both hands down, Clint cupped her buttocks in both hands and pulled her in close. The warmth of her body and the motion of her hand made his erection grow until it strained at his jeans. “Does the owner of this place know you force yourself on men this way?”

“I am the owner.”

“Oh. Well, in that case . . .” With that, Clint pulled her shirt open so he could massage her plump breasts. Danielle’s nipples were erect, and she let out a shuddering groan when he teased them between his fingers. “Is this what you were after?”

“Almost,” she replied while rubbing his groin with added vigor.

Their mouths came together for a long kiss. Somewhere along the line, Danielle ran her tongue along his lips, which sent a shiver down Clint’s spine. His hands wandered freely over her body from there, going wherever his instincts took them while roughly pulling the clothes off her body. Danielle responded in kind by unhitching Clint’s belt and pulling down his jeans before dropping to her knees in front of him.

Clint looked down at her as she took his cock into her mouth and started bobbing her head back and forth. She devoured him hungrily while moaning with pleasure as he became even harder. Every so often, she would slide her tongue all the way down his length and stay there for an extra couple of seconds.

When Clint caught his breath, he saw she was staring up at him with wide, expectant eyes. He brought her to her feet and turned her around. “What are you doing now?” she asked.

“You want me to stop,” he said while bending her over and guiding himself between her thighs, “just say so.”

Danielle grabbed the closest thing within her reach, which just happened to be a half-full barrel of oats. “Don’t you dare stop,” she said while leaning forward and taking a wider stance. When she felt Clint enter her from behind, she closed her eyes and tossed her hair back while letting out a deep moan.

Her pussy was slick and warm. Clint eased into her slowly while holding her hips in his hands. As he started to move in and out of her, he savored the feel of her tight, muscular curves and the way she adjusted to the rhythm of his thrusts. When he sped up, she rocked back and forth along with him. And when he plunged all the way into her, she groaned loudly.

Clint kept one hand on her hip and put the other on the small of her back. That way, he could feel every little shift of her backside as he pumped into her. She bent over a little more and gripped the barrel tightly so he could drive into her like a piston. Clint closed his eyes and fell into a steady motion. Her body was just the right size for him to reach forward to cup her breasts as he continued to thrust between her legs.

"Keep it up," she pleaded. "That's the—" Suddenly, Danielle's entire body tensed and she drew in a sharp breath. When she climaxed, Clint could feel her tightening around him and could hear the wood of the barrel creaking as she pressed herself against it even harder. He plunged into her once more as deep as he could, which was more than enough to send her over the edge.

Seeing her positioned in front of him with her plump backside once again in his hands was almost enough to push Clint to the edge as well. She was still moaning as he started pounding into her. He gripped her hips tightly and let his instincts tell him what to do from there and how to do it. Those instincts had never led him astray before, and they sure didn't now. Within a few more moments, he could feel his own pleasure building up inside.

Clint leaned back and drove into her one last time. He climaxed hard enough to take his breath from his lungs.

When he was able to draw another one, he realized he was gripping Danielle's hips a lot harder than he'd intended. Relaxing his hands, he rubbed her bare skin and took a step back. "Sorry about that," he said.

She straightened up and turned around to face him, naked from the waist down while lazily buttoning her shirt. "You shouldn't be. I had you pegged as a man that could curl my toes, but damn!"

"Good," Clint said. "Because I sure as hell am not sorry."

As she hiked up her jeans, Danielle wriggled her hips and smirked at him. "By the way, thanks for fetching my horse."

"And thank you for putting mine up free of charge."

"Free of charge?" As she walked past him, Danielle tapped Clint's chest. "You're gonna have to work for it, mister."

Suddenly, Clint wasn't so opposed to spending some more time in Larga Noche.

EIGHT

The sun was barely making its presence known in the western horizon when Clint returned to the Dig Dog Saloon. Although Third Avenue and Sharp Bend were considerably busier than the last time he'd been there, Leo's place had only a few more occupied tables than before. The most welcome change that Clint noticed was the stage show. A fiddler now sat beside the guitar player, and Madeline was strutting back and forth while singing a lively tune. When she saw Clint enter, she gave him a pretty smile and a nod. He acknowledged both with a tip of his hat.

Leo was still behind the bar, and even though there were less than half a dozen men standing there drinking, he acted as if he was attempting to serve the entire town. Clint chose a spot at the end of the bar farthest from the door and waited for a drink. Eventually, Leo graced him with his presence.

"I didn't think you were coming back," Leo said.

"I did my job," Clint replied.

"Exactly. So why are you here?"

"Because I only received partial payment. Gregor said you'd pay the rest upon delivery."

"Oh," Leo said with a wince. "That's right. I nearly forgot. Just a moment."

When Leo turned to head for the till, Clint said, "I'll take another beer while you're at it."

Leo removed some cash from his night's receipts and filled a mug from the tap. Handing the money over, he nervously eyed the rest of the place as though he were handling a king's ransom. Nobody else seemed to take notice, which didn't make him feel any better.

Since Clint hadn't taken the job to get rich, there wasn't much cash to count. There was enough to cover the rest of the fee he'd been promised, so he pocketed the bills and reached for the mug of beer.

"That'll be twenty-five cents," Leo said.

"What?"

"For the beer. It's twenty-five cents."

"But the first one was free," Clint pointed out.

"Right. As a thank-you for stepping in with Westin. I'm sure you'd like it if every drink was free here from now on, but that just wouldn't be good business."

"I suppose not."

"Still want that beer?"

"Sure."

As the barkeep went about a few small chores, there was a certain hunch to his back and look in his eyes that made him seem like a man bearing an excessive weight on his shoulders. Clint knew that feeling all too well. "So," he said after his next sip of beer, "what's in the bottles?"

One of Leo's eyebrows perked up, and he glanced back at him with renewed interest. "You don't really care about that."

"Sure I do."

"You stormed out of here the last time I tried to show you. Is this just your way of throwing a dog a bone?"

"My curiosity is sparked," Clint said. "I'm still here and I'd like to see what all of this effort was for, but I'm not about to beg for the privilege."

"All right. Fair enough." Leo hurried over to the shelf behind the bar, which was prominently displayed at the center of the wooden counter and just high enough to avoid being blocked by Leo's mess of red hair. He carefully took one of the bottles down and carried it over to where Clint was sitting. Lowering it behind the bar, he said, "I'm curious about something also."

"What's that?"

"When Westin was here, did you know what to expect?"

"Nope. I just got into town and it took me a hell of a lot longer to find this place than I thought it would. I saw him pushing you around and thought I could step in."

"Actually, I meant when you jumped back here where I'm standing," Leo said. "How'd you know I kept a shotgun back here?"

Clint shrugged. "I've been to more saloons than I can count. If there wasn't a shotgun somewhere back there to deal with rowdy customers, there was bound to be a club or some other such thing I could have put to use."

"Predictable, eh?"

"Fortunately, for your sake," Clint replied while lifting his glass, "yes."

"Why didn't you just draw your pistol?"

"Are all these questions necessary just for me to see that bottle? If so, I think I'll finish my beer in peace and allow my curiosity to fade on its own."

"No, I'm just curious as well," Leo said as he placed the bottle on the bar. "A man in my line of work sometimes runs afoul of characters like Westin. I just thought it might help if I could learn whatever might—"

Since Leo seemed serious about wanting to know and

didn't seem ready to stop talking anytime soon, Clint said, "Intimidation."

"You don't think a pistol would have been enough?"

"Obviously your man Westin wasn't the sort to be swayed by threats or just another gun being waved at him. Damn near any man tends to think twice when he's on the wrong end of a scattergun. At the very least, it makes him stop what he's doing for a spell."

"And what if there had just been a club or something like that under here?"

Clint answered that by patting the gun on his hip.

"I see," Leo said.

"So," Clint said, "does all of that grant me the answer to my original question or do I have to wait some more?"

Leo flinched as if he'd forgotten completely about the bottle in front of him. "Oh, yes! This bottle contains one of my finest ideas in regard to my business to date."

"You own this place outright?"

"The Dog? Naturally."

"And you expect a new brand of liquor to bring people in by the cartload?"

"Not just a new brand," Leo declared proudly. "It's a rare delicacy imported from across the ocean!" Uncorking the bottle, he poured half a splash into a small glass and handed it to Clint. "When it becomes known that I'm serving this, I might as well print my own supply of money."

Clint took the glass, sniffed it, and wondered if Leo was crazy or if it would be even more insane to drink something that nearly singed the hairs in his nose after just one sniff.

NINE

Clint wasn't the sort of man who drank himself into a stupor at every opportunity, but he was no stranger to the contents of most of the bottles he could see behind Leo's bar. Since he'd already come this far, he decided to confirm his suspicion by accepting the drink he'd been given. Clint tossed it back, set the glass down, and waited for the fire to work itself all the way down to his belly.

All the while, Leo watched as if he were witnessing a miracle. "Well?" he asked before he busted at the seams. "What do you think?"

"I think it's vodka."

"That may be one word for it, but I assure you this is something altogether—"

"No," Clint cut in through a hacking cough. "It's potent, I'll grant you that much. But it's vodka."

"And how would you know?"

"Because I've had it before."

Leo picked up the bottle and scrutinized the label, which was written in another language beneath a black drawing of a wolf's head. "This is just wonderful. Then again, the way things have been going, why should I have expected anything different?"

"Did Gregor tell you he made this stuff?" Clint asked.

"No."

"Did he say it could only be found in some far corner of the globe?"

"No," Leo sighed. "Just that it's supposed to be rare."

"He wasn't altogether wrong about that," Clint said.

"But you just said you've had it before."

"I have. That doesn't mean I've been able to find it in every saloon I've ever visited." He actually hadn't looked for it at any other saloons, but Clint decided to keep that bit of information to himself.

Judging by the glimmer in Leo's eye, that was the right decision. "So it *is* rare?"

"I suppose so."

"Gregor also told me that it's from one of the finest distilleries in Europe."

"Could be." Clint lifted the glass to his nose and took a cautious sniff. "Mind if I have another sample?"

Leo practically beamed with a smile as he poured the drink. Not only did he seem happy about doing so, but he gave Clint almost twice the amount he'd had before. He then watched as Clint brought the glass to his lips and took a slower taste. While Clint sampled the liquor, Leo drummed his fingers like an expectant father waiting to find out if he was going to have a new son or daughter. When he couldn't stand any more, he asked, "Well? What do you think?"

"I think it's very good," Clint replied in a voice that he strained to push out. Even before he'd finished that sentence, he could feel the effect the liquor was having on him. "What . . ." He had to stop to cough a few times into his hand. "What makes you think this will be such a moneymaker?"

"Because it's different!" Leaning with his elbow on the bar, Leo said, "Running a saloon is a difficult trade. The ones that survive are the ones that have something good to offer. Something folks can't get anywhere else."

"Like vodka?"

"For a start."

"Then won't you need more than three bottles?"

"Eventually. What's important at the start is for me to have something that no other saloon in this town has. Fact is, no other saloon in any town throughout this county serves this fine vintage."

"I thought vintages were just for wine," Clint said.

Leo dismissed that with a wave of his hand. "Doesn't matter," he said. "I've been working on an advertisement that will let everyone know how rare and exotic this fine drink is and they'll have to come here to get it. Even if someplace like the Tiger's Paw or Mackie's gets their hands on a few bottles, they won't be able to get anything of this quality!"

"Before you put something in print, are you certain this is as rare as you think?"

"Of course. I visited dozens of saloons throughout New Mexico and only found one place that served anything like this. Well . . . maybe two. Anyway, what they served was absolute swill compared to this."

Clint looked at the glass and then the bottle without figuring out how either that liquor or the man serving it could accomplish such feats. Since that wasn't his concern, he shrugged his shoulders and turned to get a look at the stage. "Tell me about Madeline," he said.

"Ah, yes. She's another one of my exclusive attractions."

"I can imagine."

When Leo laughed, it was a grating combination of a grunt and a cough. To make it even worse, he added a nudge from his elbow. "Not that sort of attraction, although I imagine she is quite extraordinary in that regard." He could only maintain his leering grin for a few seconds before adding, "She's just here to sing. She truly is a delightful girl."

One thing that did separate Leo's place from so many others was the bit of genuine affection its owner showed to a pretty girl who worked there. That kind of change did Clint some good to see.

"She used to sing in some of the largest halls in New York City, you know," Leo said.

"Is that so?"

"Yep. That's what she told me."

"And how'd you get her out here?" Clint asked.

"I paid her way and matched the pay she was getting back East." Leo dropped his voice to a whisper and nudged Clint some more. "I actually did some dealing to lower her price."

"Was she worth it?"

"I don't know. You tell me."

Once again, when Clint was expecting something slimy from the barkeep, he was pleasantly surprised. Instead of being offered to spend any private time with her, he was directed to the stage, where Madeline was about to sing. After pointing in that direction, Leo settled in by leaning against the bar like he was just another customer getting ready to enjoy the show.

"You seem like a nice enough fellow, Leo," Clint said.

"I appreciate that."

"A little misguided, but your heart's in the right place."

Leo smiled in preparation to graciously receive that before Clint's words truly sank in. "Wait a second. Misguided?"

"Seems that way, yeah. And I'm doing you the favor of telling you straight out."

"Umm . . . thanks."

"You're looking to improve your saloon? It'll take more than a few bottles of expensive liquor."

"I know," Leo replied. "I've got other plans, too, you know."

"Do any of those plans include a new name for the place?"

"No. Why? You don't like the Dog?"

"The Dog would be an improvement," Clint said. "What the hell is the Dig Dog supposed to be?"

"It used to be the Digging Dog, but the fellow who painted the sign on the front window got sick and never came back."

Clint looked at him without blinking for a few seconds. Onstage, Madeline launched into a bouncy tune that got about four of the customers to look up from what they were doing. Suddenly, he wondered why he'd even started the conversation in the first place.

"The name's fine," Clint said. "Whatever trips your trigger."

"What should I change it to?"

"Come to think of it, you've got bigger problems than that."

When he heard that, Leo seemed even more upset than when he'd been pulled off his feet and dragged over the bar by the front of his shirt. "What's that supposed to mean?"

"What was that Westin fella after?"

Although he was still upset, Leo closed up tighter than a frozen clam. "Never you mind about that."

"Come on now," Clint prodded. "After I put my neck on the line, I don't even get to know what it was all about?"

"No."

"Come on."

"What do you care?" Leo snapped.

Clint leaned back against the bar with his beer and

listened to Madeline sing. He couldn't decide whether staying in Larga Noche would be a colossal waste of time or one hell of a business opportunity. After thinking back to the talk he'd just had with Leo, his decision was that much easier to make. Come morning, he would toss a saddle onto Eclipse's back and get the hell out of there. For now, he had a beer to finish.

TEN

By the time Clint managed to stagger out of the Dig Dog Saloon and navigate the nonsensical streets of Larga Noche, he wanted to get out of town even more. Unfortunately, he'd gotten involved in a card game that had lasted well into the night. That, combined with the other drinks he'd had along the way, made it a bad idea to do any riding just yet. Taking the small bit of money he'd won at poker, Clint found a small hotel at the southern end of Linden Street.

"What time is it?" he asked the desk clerk while signing the hotel's register.

"Ten thirty."

"Is that all? Are you sure?"

The clerk was a tall fellow with a thick head of gray hair. He nodded and chewed on the stub of a cigar that hung from one corner of his mouth like a root. "I am, Mr. Abrams. Got me a new watch and everything."

"Adams. The name's Adams."

"Looks like Abrams on the register there."

"It isn't."

The clerk examined Clint's signature and gave up the

meaningless argument with a shrug. He reached out with the key in his hand, but rather than waiting for Clint to take it, he dropped it onto the desk.

Standing there with his hand outstretched, Clint grumbled, "I hate this damn town."

"What was that?" the clerk mumbled.

"Nothing."

"Oh. Good night, then."

Clint's room was at the top of a small flight of stairs. He unlocked the door, tossed his saddlebags into a corner, and sat down on the bed. Leo's expensive liquor was still causing parts of Clint's brain to throb, and when he closed his eyes, the sensation turned into a pleasant, gentle spinning. Naturally, as soon as he started to truly relax, someone knocked on the door.

For a few seconds, Clint lay on top of his blankets, still wearing his boots, and tried to convince himself he hadn't heard a thing.

The knock came again.

"Didn't hear it," Clint sighed.

When it came again, Clint jumped out of bed and marched all three steps required to get to the door. He pulled it open, ready to demand an explanation from whoever was on the other side, when he was cut off by a sharp punch to the mouth.

"That's for you stickin' yer nose where it didn't belong back at that saloon," Westin said while shoving Clint backward.

Every one of Clint's senses was overpowered by the surprise blow to his face. He wasn't completely overwhelmed, but the effect lasted just long enough for Westin and two other men to step into his room and shut the door behind them.

Although neither of the other two men was as large as

Westin, they came awfully close. The closest one to him in height had a thick stump of a neck connected to a fleshy bald head. The other had a long, narrow face with sunken features partially obscured by stubble. He wore his pistol in a cross-draw holster located on the same side of his body as the pinned-up sleeve where his right arm should have been.

Clint eased his hand down to his side just to make sure the Colt was there. It wasn't. Only when he felt the jolt of his blood pumping a little faster through him did he remember unbuckling the gun belt and dropping it on top of his saddlebags before stretching out on the bed. While that meant the Colt was out of the intruders' sight, it also meant it was out of his reach for the moment.

This had to be the first time in quite a while that he'd answered the door of his hotel room without a gun in his hand. He vowed that would never happen again. Forgetting who he was—that he was the Gunsmith—could well end up getting him killed one day.

"Who the hell are you?" Clint asked. "And what the hell do you want?"

"I'm Westin Voss. We already met. That there is Kurt," he said while pointing to the bald man, "and that's Samuel," he said as he nodded at the one-armed man. "No need for you to introduce yourself. I already know you're Clint Adams."

"So you can read a hotel register," Clint said. "Am I supposed to be impressed? Then again, by the looks of you three, I suppose I am impressed that even one of you can read."

Kurt stepped forward with a surprising amount of speed for a man of his size. His right fist caught Clint in the stomach with a low uppercut. Even though Clint reflexively tensed to absorb the blow, he could still feel the impact roll through his body. Kurt's cruel smile made it clear that he knew the effects of the blow well enough.

Focusing all of the rage that boiled up from his aching torso, Clint glared first at Kurt and then at Westin. "You were awfully quick to answer the first question. What about the second?"

Westin's eyes narrowed as he took a moment to study Clint's face. When he was through, he stalked forward and grabbed Clint's collar. Clint's response was to take a swing at him, but the effort was stopped by a chopping punch to his ribs just beneath his arm. Kurt's fist landed in a spot that put a haze behind Clint's eyes and robbed him of the strength to finish the punch he'd started.

All this time, Westin stood still without the first hint of fear that he might get hit somewhere along the way. "You're a friend of that barkeep," he said. "You know goddamn well why I was there."

"I only just met Leo," Clint said.

"Then how do you know his name?" Kurt asked.

"Do you know Abraham Lincoln's name?"

Kurt recoiled, scowled, and then replied, "Yeah. Who doesn't?"

"Then he must be a friend of yours, right?" Even though he figured a snide grin would buy him another punch from the bald man, Clint simply couldn't resist. He was correct in that assumption, but at least Kurt's next blow landed just a bit lower than the first.

Clint went limp and hacked up a rough breath. He could take that punch and plenty more, but his best bet was to let the other men think they were knocking him around harder than they were so they'd relax their guard a bit.

"Talk some sense into that barkeep friend of yours," Westin said. "If he ain't a friend, then try to talk some sense into him anyway."

"It might help if I knew what you were talking about."

"The whore he's got working for him."

"Leo has whores working at the Dog?"

"It's a saloon, ain't it?" Westin spat. "Every saloon's got whores working in 'em."

"What's this one's name?"

Perhaps on his own accord or perhaps due to an unseen signal from Westin, Kurt slammed his fist into Clint's stomach. Since he hadn't seen that one coming, Clint wasn't able to tense. He let out a grunt that brought up some of his last meal along with it. When Westin and Kurt started to laugh while looking down at the mess on the floor, Clint pulled away from them with all the strength he could dredge up.

Clint's shirt tore away, leaving Westin with a tattered portion of collar in his hand. Knowing how quickly Kurt could move, Clint made him his next priority by delivering a powerful right cross to the bald man's chin. That sent Kurt staggering backward and gave Clint a small window of opportunity to move around his bed and pick up the Colt. The gun belt was in his sight less than an inch away from his extended fingers when Clint heard the distinctive sounds of a pistol clearing leather and a hammer being thumbed back.

Glancing toward the door, Clint saw that Samuel was the one who'd gotten to his pistol and was aiming it directly at him. He may have had only one arm, but it was a mighty capable one.

"I see you still got some fight in ya," Westin said as he walked over and shoved Clint aside. "That won't last much longer."

ELEVEN

It was early afternoon the following day when Clint stepped through the Big Dog's batwing doors again. He was already starting to recognize the faces of some of the saloon's regular customers scattered among spots at the card tables and bar. The few of them that looked back at him did so with startled expressions on their faces. Considering the state he was in, Clint couldn't exactly blame them.

There was someone else behind the bar this time. She was a short woman with a stout build. As he approached, Clint looked her up and down. She showed him a nervous smile while tending to a few stray strands of her light brown hair.

"Anything I can do for you, mister?" she asked.

"Where's Leo?" Clint replied.

"Mr. Parker? He's not here. Tell me what you need and I can try to help you."

The woman was more than a full head shorter than him, yet she carried herself like someone who could look directly into anyone's eyes. Judging by the modest dress she wore and the simple manner in which she kept her hair, Clint doubted she was the woman Westin was after. "I need to have a word with Leo."

Settling in as if to let him know she wasn't about to budge, the woman said, "I'm the one who can help you with that, so why don't you do something for me."

"What?"

"Tell me why you're looking me over like a slab of meat in a butcher's window. I know I'm a breathtaking sight, but it's been some years since I've captured a man's eye like this."

Clint couldn't help but smile. The expression sent jabs of pain through his jaw all the way up to his eye sockets. "Sorry. I had a hell of a night."

"I can tell. You look like a man who was either in a fight or slammed his face in a door."

"It'd be nice if it was just my face."

She laughed and turned around toward the shelves of liquor behind the bar. "Let me get something to help ease the pain a bit."

"Don't bother pouring me any of that expensive firewater I dragged all the way out here."

"Wouldn't dream of it," the woman said in a tone that was soothing despite being more than a little rough around the edges. "I've got some coffee with a little bit of a surprise for you."

"What kind of surprise?" Clint asked.

"Probably best you didn't know," she told him while pouring a few splashes from several smaller bottles into a mug.

Since it hurt for him to keep his eyes all the way open for too long, Clint didn't bother trying to see what she was concocting for him.

"Why don't you have a seat?" she said. "I'll bring it to you."

"Don't mind if I do." As long as Clint maintained a certain somewhat crooked posture, his ribs didn't ache as badly. His back cramped from the fitful night of sleep he'd had and his face . . . well, there wasn't much that could be done for his face.

When the woman approached the table he'd chosen, she seemed even smaller in stature than he'd originally guessed. She approached him and set the mug down in front of him. "There you go," she said. "Sip, don't gulp."

Clint held the mug in his hands so the warmth could soak into his skin. Although the mug's contents smelled vaguely of coffee, there was a strange mix of other scents in there as well. Something in there was spicy enough to reach all the way down to his throat through his nose. "I'll give it my best," he said while tentatively bringing the mug to his lips.

The coffee portion of the drink was strong. Whatever the rest of it was, it created a warmth in his mouth that had nothing to do with the actual heat of the liquid. A peppery flavor stuck to his tongue without scalding it, and as the mixture went down, it soothed his innards like a warm bath would have soothed his muscles. A second sip made his head feel better than it had all day, and when he lifted the mug for a third sip, he felt a strong hand on his arm holding it in place.

"Remember," the woman warned. "Sip."

Oddly enough, Clint had been fully prepared to down the rest of that coffee in one last gulp. He nodded and took a restrained sip instead. After swallowing it, he told her, "Thanks."

"Anytime," she said. "You look like you need more than this, though. Have you seen a doctor?"

"Don't need a doctor."

"Let me bring you a mirror. One look into that and you might feel differently."

"I already know what to expect on that account. This isn't exactly the first time I'd have seen that particular sight."

"Such a shame. You seem like a nice gentleman."

"And you," Clint said while holding up the mug of modified coffee, "are a godsend."

"Just Henrietta," she told him. "Or if you insist," she added with a wink, "Saint Henrietta. I'll be over at the bar if you need me. But don't ask for another cup of that special coffee. Only one serving every twelve hours unless you want to go blind."

Clint laughed at that, but quickly realized he was the only one. Henrietta either had a very good poker face or she hadn't been kidding about him going blind from drinking too much of her mixture. Whichever it was, Clint continued sipping from the mug and rubbing his temples.

After a few minutes of silently cursing the saloon's guitar player for continuing to play, Clint was joined by the owner of the Dig Dog.

Leo sat down across from him and took a sip from the cup he'd brought along. After a second or two, he said, "You look like hell."

"Really?" Clint grunted. "I hadn't noticed."

"What happened?"

Clint looked up at him and replied, "Someone paid me a visit. I'll give you one guess who it was."

"Westin," Leo sighed.

"You got it."

"I was afraid of that."

"Well, a word of warning might have been helpful," Clint said before taking another sip of Henrietta's miracle brew.

"I swear I didn't think something like this would happen. I mean, there was always the chance of him coming back here, but that seemed fairly obvious."

"I want you to tell me what this is about," Clint said. "I

asked before and allowed you to dance around the subject because it is, after all, your business. But since I've been dragged into this, I'm making it my business as well."

"I'll tell you," Leo said quietly. "I owe you that much. But first, tell me one thing. That man over at the table behind you. The one facing the bar. Do you recognize him?"

Clint turned, looked, and almost didn't recognize Samuel sitting there with his head bowed and his face mostly covered by the wide brim of his hat. As soon as he knew for certain that it was him, Clint gripped the sides of his table and started to stand up. He wanted to put that one-armed bastard down, even if he had to burn the Dig Dog to cinders to do it.

TWELVE

Leo's hand snapped out to grab Clint's shoulder and push him down. If Clint hadn't been in such rough shape from the night before, the barkeep never would have been able to do it.

"If you don't let go of me," Clint snarled, "you'll lose that hand of yours."

"You've obviously met that one, Clint. He's been watching this place and you've got to know he can gun you down before you make it halfway to his table."

"Not if I shoot him from here."

"I'll not have you turn my place into a slaughterhouse. Now if you want them answers, you'll follow me to where we can speak in private."

Leo then let go of Clint's shoulder, stood up, and walked toward a narrow door near the back end of the bar marked PRIVATE. When he stood up, Clint's hand twitched toward the Colt at his side. His eyes shot daggers into the man sitting on the other side of the room, and every fiber of his body wanted nothing more than to cross that room and knock Samuel's head from his shoulders.

"Not a good idea, friend," Henrietta said from a few paces away.

Clint shifted his eyes toward her. When he saw her looking up at him, he couldn't help but relax a bit. "How do you know what ideas are in my head?" he asked.

"Near as I can figure, there's only one at the moment, and it ends with me having to help clean up another mess in this place."

He let out a sigh. "Doctor and fortune-teller, huh? Why waste your talents tending bar?"

"Free drinks."

Somehow, the rest of Clint's anger drained away. He knew it would return easily enough if Samuel looked at him for too long, but the one-armed man seemed to be wrapped up in his game.

"Here," Henrietta said while handing Clint a mug that was less than a quarter full.

He took it, sniffed its contents, and smiled. "I thought you said I was only allowed one helping every twelve hours."

"You're in worse shape than most of my patients. Just don't even try to convince me to make any more for a while."

"Saint Henrietta," was all Clint needed to say as he accepted the mug and allowed the one-armed man to keep his teeth for one more day.

On the other side of the door Leo had used was a modest office complete with the wooden frame of a small cot and a round table with a washbasin on it that was drier than the desert floor. Leo sat next to a little desk that seemed ready to collapse beneath the weight of all the disorganized papers stacked on top of it. "If you want to put this place on the map," Clint said as he made his way to the cot frame, "put that woman in charge."

"You mean Henrietta?"

"Whatever you're paying her isn't enough."

Leo nodded halfheartedly and stood up. "That man out there works with Westin Voss."

"I put that together already."

"So was it him that did that to you?" the barkeep asked while nervously waving a hand to indicate Clint's battered face.

"Him, Westin, and some bald ape with a thick neck."

"That'd be Kurt."

"Yes, it would. Westin said he wanted me to have a word with you."

"About what?" Leo asked.

"Don't try to sound innocent," Clint said as he took a breath that he felt all the way down to the pit of his stomach. He tried to keep from wincing, but the stabbing pain in his ribs made that next to impossible. "Westin said you'd know what he was after, and I'm inclined to believe him."

"When you came along yesterday, Westin was trying to get me to pay him a sum of money that he says is owed to him."

"For what?"

"For being a Voss."

Clint took a sip from the mug Henrietta had given him. After the brew had helped ease some of the pain rolling through his body, he asked, "He's some important man in this town?"

"Not really, but his father had an eye for land speculation that allowed him to pull together enough money for a comfortable living. When the old man died, he left just enough to Westin for him to buy a new horse and a secondhand saddle."

"How do you know so much about all of this?" Clint asked, already dreading the answer.

"Because that old man was my father, too."

Clint swore under his breath. There were a few kinds of

fights that were best viewed from a distance. Those on a battlefield and those between brothers. "So Westin Voss is your kin?"

"We're stepbrothers. His father took me in when I was eight. I'd lost my parents and . . . well . . . it's a long story, but the short of it is that me and Westin grew up together."

"You were close?"

"Close?" Leo asked with a chuckle. "Westin started off hating me and only grew to hate me more. See, the old man always wanted to pass along his business to his family. He would always take Westin aside and try to teach him, but Westin wouldn't have any of it. As he grew older, Westin became . . . pretty much what you've seen. He struck out on his own when he was seventeen and would only show up at home when he needed money or at one of the old man's properties when he needed a place to lay low for whatever reason."

"But the old man got along with you, right?"

"Yes," Leo replied softly. "But it felt more like a friendship. A strained one at best. Westin hated him for it. He hated me worse."

"So Westin is after a piece of his inheritance," Clint said.

"That's right. The only problem is that there isn't one to be had."

THIRTEEN

"There's nothing left?" Clint asked.

"That's right."

"So why don't you just tell that to Westin?"

"I did!" Leo said. "That was the first thing I told him, in fact, and he didn't believe me. The last time he saw the old man was years ago and there was still a big family spread, horses, and plenty of money to go around. But property speculation, especially when it involves mining claims and dealing with the railroads, can be—"

"Tricky," Clint finished for him.

"At best. By the time the old man passed on, he was close to broke. Fact is, that's probably what drove him into the grave in the first place."

"How could Westin not know about any of that?" Clint asked.

"When I say Westin left home, I mean it in every sense of the word. He was gone and didn't give a damn about what happened while he was away. When he came back, he stuck his hand out and said whatever he needed to for someone to put a few dollars into it. Then he rode off to rob or carouse or whatever else he did. Honestly, I never knew exactly what he got up to. I was just glad he was gone."

Clint noticed that the expression on Leo's face was similar to that of a dog that had been whipped for most of its life. His eyes never stayed in one place for long, and his head's natural position was at a slightly downward angle.

"When we were boys," Leo continued, "Westin never missed a chance to knock me down or bloody my nose. As we got older, I thought things would get better. That was foolish. He just grew stronger and carried a gun. One time when he came home, he saw how much closer me and the old man had gotten. He cornered me one night and beat the tar out of me. At one point, I swore he was going to kill me. The next day, he apologized and blamed it on him being drunk." Leo shook his head as he stared at a point far beyond that office. "But I know it was more than that."

"What was your father's name?" Clint asked.

Although he seemed grateful to talk about something else, Leo was also confused. "His name?"

"Yes. All I've ever heard you call him is the old man."

As soon as he saw the shadow fall over Leo's face, Clint knew why he hadn't heard the elder Voss's name.

"Jarrett," Leo said as if he'd just heard about his stepfather's death. "His name was Jarrett. He was a good man. Even though he never truly looked at me with pride or compassion, I know he thought of me as a . . . well . . . that he cared."

"I'm sure he wouldn't have wanted any of this to happen between you and Westin."

"He knew the two of us butted heads. He always just told me we'd work things out eventually."

"Can you appeal to some of the other family members?" Clint asked. "Maybe get some sort of proof that you don't have the money Westin is after?"

"It won't matter. I already told him that right before you walked in. He wasn't interested in what was left over or what I might have. He wants to take everything from me, plain and simple, and I doubt he'll be happy with just money."

"What is he trying to get from you?"

"Well, money is a part of it, that's for certain," Leo admitted. "Whatever sum I was willing to pay, he wanted more. Knowing him the way I do, I can tell you that even if I came up with that new sum, he'd tack more onto it. What he really wants is Madeline."

Clint laughed. "Can't he just come to watch her sing?"

"That's not it. He wants me to hand her over to him."

Any trace of humor on Clint's face disappeared when he heard that. "What?"

Leo drew a deep breath and let it out in a labored sigh. "He wants me to draw up a contract with her that ties her to me legally so I can then hand her over to him."

"You mean like a slave?"

"I mean like a whore. There are plenty of soiled doves who accept money in advance to pay for them to come out West or to a different city or even to a different country. In exchange, they're required to work off their debt in any number of ways. On paper, it's all spelled out in prettier language but it all boils down to the same thing."

"You seem to know quite a lot about this sort of thing," Clint said.

"I've discovered many unsavory kinds of men making offers for various goods and services to be featured in my saloon. Men like that make the rounds, peddling everything from women to opium and—"

"And vodka?"

"If you're thinking of Gregor, I can put your mind at ease. I've dealt with him for years, and the reason for that is because he's got scruples. He may work in some shady areas, but he's an angel compared to the scum that try to shackle young ladies with contracts and threats of violence."

"That's good to hear," Clint said. "Because it's my experience that scum of that sort usually come to a bad end."

"Them or the people around them," Leo replied. He stood up, walked over to one of the dusty boxes piled in a corner, and removed a slightly less dusty bottle. "When I got into this business, it was to put some of what I'd learned from the old man to good use without dealing in the cutthroat circles that he did. I won't say that running a saloon is as risky as what he did, but it's a much more difficult trade than I imagined."

Clint stood as well, mostly because sitting on the cot frame was playing hell with his already aching bones. "Tell me what Westin proposed exactly."

"I didn't ask you back here to heap my problems onto you. I wanted to thank you for stepping in the way you already have and repay your kindness as best I can." Brushing off the label stuck to the bottle in his hand, Leo treated it as a collector might treat a fine work of art. "This here wine is older than the both of us, and I'm guessing it came from a much fancier house than we've ever lived in. Take it," he said while handing it over.

Clint took the bottle just to get a look at it. The label was in French, and the cork was sealed in place with dark red wax. "I'm not much of a wine drinker," he said.

"You can sell it for a mighty healthy profit. It'll have to be in a town bigger than this one, but I can think of a handful of merchants in Gregor's neck of the woods that would be willing to let you name your price. I'd give you more, but that's the last bottle I have, and the last thing I own that's worth much of anything."

"What about the vodka?"

"You want one of those bottles?"

"No. I mean why bother with the vodka when you've got something like this to draw a crowd?"

Leo laughed. "Have you ever tried to serve wine to a bunch of dusty cowboys and ranch hands?"

"No," Clint replied.

"Well, I have and it ain't pretty. They demanded something with kick, and I'm hoping what you brought from Gregor will be just the thing."

"I appreciate it, but I was just doing the job you and Gregor hired me to do."

"Keep the wine," Leo insisted. "You earned it."

"I will, but I haven't earned it yet. Tell me everything about Westin's demands," Clint said.

Leo looked at him suspiciously. "Why?"

"Because the only thing worse than giving in to a spoiled brother's tantrum is harming a woman as fine as Madeline."

"I agree."

"So let's do something about it."

FOURTEEN

An hour or so later, Clint emerged from Leo's office. He went straight to Henrietta and asked, "Where can I find Madeline?"

"Probably in her house," the short woman replied.

"Where's that?"

"If I had a dime every time a man asked me that same question, I'd be a very wealthy woman."

"When will she be back here again?" Clint asked.

"She's supposed to sing tonight around eight."

"Tell me one thing at least. Wherever Madeline is, is she safe?"

Henrietta thought about that. "She's a good girl, Mr. Adams. I won't do anything to bring her to harm." Lowering her voice so as not to attract much attention, she added, "I've heard about Westin's intentions toward her, and even he's not stupid enough to track her down and kidnap the poor thing."

After all the mad dogs and bad men that had crossed Clint's path over the years, he doubted that very much.

"I've made it my business to keep an eye on her,"

Henrietta continued. "And if I find even the slightest cause for alarm, I'll let you know. How'd that be?"

"That would be just fine. I'm staying in a hotel down on Linden Street at the south end of town."

"I know the place."

"I'll be there in a short while, and I'll come back here to see Madeline sing."

"I'll tell her you're coming." Henrietta reached up to gently pat Clint's swollen cheek. She clucked like a mother hen while fussing with some strands of hair that had stuck to the dried blood on one of his cuts. "You've got to see a doctor."

"I've had worse."

"You'll also get another batch of my coffee when you come back. Until then, try to get some rest. Is that a deal?"

"Yes, ma'am."

"Good. Now I've got work to do." With that, she turned her back on him and was immediately flagged down by one of the other customers.

Clint couldn't help but notice how the folks in that saloon responded to her. Every one of them seemed anxious to catch her eye and hear what she had to say. For the first time since he'd arrived, the Dig Dog seemed like a proper saloon where folks wanted to be instead of being stuck there because they were too drunk to walk away.

As soon as he stepped outside, Clint pulled in a breath of fresh air. There was something about the dry desert winds that soothed a man from the inside out. He wasn't sure how much stock he put in those who said climate could cure everything from consumption to black lung, but it sure did wonders for a man's spirit. In that single breath, Clint could smell a few different flowers while also savoring the sun's rays in a way that was distinct to the desert. He pushed his luck, however, by inhaling deeply enough to swell his chest to the point of straining his tender ribs. The breath that had started out so nicely was ended with a series of wheezing coughs as Clint walked slowly toward Third Avenue.

Although stretching his legs didn't do much to soothe his aching body, it allowed Clint to focus his thoughts on the task at hand like sunlight being narrowed to a burning ray through the lens of a magnifying glass. Every bit of pain he felt made him think that much harder about what he and Leo had discussed. That kind of focus took its toll, however. By the time he arrived at the stable where Eclipse was boarded, he felt as if he'd walked a few miles just to get there.

The Darley Arabian stallion noticed Clint as soon as he entered the drafty barn. Stepping up to place his chest against the lowest section of his stall, Eclipse waited for him to come over and rub his nose.

"How you doing, boy?" Clint asked as he scratched the horse's muzzle and neck. "Are you getting the royal treatment?"

"His owner didn't exactly pay for the royal treatment," Danielle said as she walked in through the back door, "but I doubt he's got any complaints. Ain't that right, big boy?"

Eclipse was quick to turn away from Clint to receive some affection from the curvy woman tending to him. Danielle wore her thick brown hair in pigtails that day to keep it out of her face. Her plain red shirt was tied at the midsection, and even though she wore a thin white undershirt beneath it, the lines of her body could still be clearly seen thanks to the sweat from her skin. She turned toward Clint and raised her eyebrows. "I was gonna say that your horse was getting treated better than you, but now I see that's even more true than I thought. What on earth happened to you?"

"I tripped over a loose floorboard."

"Unless you tripped through a third-floor window, I doubt that very much."

"If you don't mind, I'd rather not talk about it," Clint said. "I just came by to throw a saddle on Eclipse and take a ride."

"You need to see a doctor."

"Why does everyone keep saying that?" Almost as soon as those words came out of him, Clint added, "Don't answer that. I don't need a doctor. I'll be fine."

"What happens if you fall from your saddle when you're out there alone somewhere?"

"This boy has plenty of tricks up his sleeve," Clint said as he patted the side of Eclipse's neck. "He'll come up with something."

"If you're too stupid to go to a doctor in the shape you're in, then at least let me ride along with you. That mare over yonder could use a good run."

While Clint wasn't the sort who was quick to accept pity, he would have been truly stupid to pass up an offer like that from a woman like Danielle. Even if he'd had any argument against her coming along, it wouldn't have lasted long when he saw her lean over a gate into another stall to retrieve her saddle. Knowing full well that he'd been enjoying the sight of her backside, Danielle turned and asked, "Are you going to help me with this?"

"I don't believe I've got a choice."

"Damn right you don't!"

FIFTEEN

When Clint had first thought about taking a ride to clear his head, it had seemed like a good idea. When Danielle wanted to join him, it seemed like an even better idea. As far as his injuries went, he figured he'd stop feeling them after a while if he just kept riding and let his mind drift in other directions. That last part couldn't have been more wrong.

He pulled back on his reins, bringing Eclipse to a stop about a mile outside of town. "What's the matter?" Danielle asked. "Are you feeling all right?"

"I'm fine," Clint lied. "This just looks like a good spot."

Fortunately, the spot he'd randomly chosen did have its merits. Just off the trail was a wide field of tall grass beneath a wide, bright blue sky. "You're right," she said. "And there's a stream right over there where we can water the horses."

"Perfect. Let's do that."

They dismounted, led two grateful horses to a shallow stream, and found a clear spot where Clint could lay out the blanket he'd brought. He then eased himself down so he could sit and try not to grunt too loudly with the effort of it all.

"You sure you're all right?" Danielle asked. "That sounded like you just aged twenty years when you sat down."

"Respect your elders, girl," Clint grunted.

She moved closer to him on both knees and began tugging at his shirt. Although her efforts weren't completely unwanted, he shifted and tried to steer her away from the buttons she'd been fussing with. "I didn't think this would be so difficult," she said.

"Then maybe you should—"

"Good Lord!" Danielle gasped. "What happened to you and don't you dare feed me some kind of story."

Clint thought of a few jokes he could make, but once he looked down at his heavily bruised ribs, he knew they wouldn't go over well. "It looks worse than it is," he explained.

Running her hands gently over the mottled patches of dark blue, black, and red, she said, "Well, that's not saying much. If it was as bad as it looked, you wouldn't be able to walk. Somebody did this to you."

"What makes you say that?"

"The fist marks right there and there." When she pointed them out, Danielle poked Clint's side as if she was trying to push him over.

"All right, all right! You got me," Clint said. "Just for the love of God, stop that!"

Keeping her finger poised over one of the darkest bruises, she scowled at him and asked, "What happened to you?"

"I got the hell beat out of me."

"Tell me you gave as good as you got."

"I did my best."

"That wasn't very convincing," she said.

"There were three of them."

As soon as he saw the reaction he got from Danielle, Clint added, "Three of them with guns."

"Oh my God. I'm sorry I gave you such a hard time."

"I should think so."

She moved in closer to him while reaching out with cautious hands. Placing one hand upon his ribs, she asked, "Does this hurt?"

"A little."

Danielle smirked since she knew he was playing up the situation, but she went along with it for the moment. "What about this?" she asked while rubbing her other hand against his chest.

"Not as much," Clint said.

She took the hand from his ribs and brushed it against his face. When he winced dramatically, she said, "Oh, come on. Don't be such a little daisy."

"Daisy?" Clint said. "Is that what you think?" He proved his point by using one hand to pull her face close enough to his for him to plant a kiss on her that lasted a good long while. Partway through it, Danielle slipped her tongue into his mouth and let her hands wander down along his body.

Drawing in a sharp, sudden breath, Clint said, "Okay, now that really did hurt a bit."

She was touching one of the more heavily bruised parts of his torso and quickly pulled her hand back. "Sorry about that."

Clint stretched out his legs and lay back with his hands clasped behind his head. "I suppose you'll just have to make it up to me somehow."

Slowly crawling on top of him, Danielle was careful not to put any pressure on his upper body. Instead, she straddled the lower portion of his hips while tugging at Clint's belt buckle. "I think I might be able to come up with something," she said. Before long, she'd loosened his jeans and peeled them off him.

The moment she'd started touching him, Clint could feel his body responding to her. By the time her hand found his cock, it had become fully erect. She stroked it with one hand before wrapping her lips around its tip. He looked down to watch her lick him as if she was savoring a cool piece of ice on a hot summer day. Her eyes wandered up to meet his as she opened her mouth and took him all the way in. Closing her lips around the base of his shaft, she started slowly bobbing up and down.

Before long, Clint couldn't help but squirm. He reached down to put his hands on her head to keep her in the right spot at some times and to urge her to suck him harder at others. Danielle responded to every one of his requests while teasing him with her tongue. Just beforc he reached the point of no return, she lifted her head and asked, "Is that enough for you to forgive me?"

"Not quite," he told her.

She smiled hungrily while stripping out of her clothes. "I was hoping you'd say that."

Clint enjoyed watching her remove every layer of her clothing until she was stark naked. Standing over him, Danielle ran her hands over her ample breasts. Slowly, she straddled him and lowered herself down onto his rigid pole. She reached down to guide him between her legs. When Clint was finally inside her, they both let out long, grateful moans.

He reached up to hold her hips as she began to rock back and forth. Lost in the moment, she placed her hands upon his chest and leaned forward. Danielle's eyes snapped open when she heard Clint suck in a painful breath. "Sorry," she said.

Rather than saying anything, he used one hand to pull her down so he could kiss her long and hard. His other hand gripped her backside to hold her in place as he started pumping up into her. Danielle may have been surprised by his show of initiative, but she wasn't about to complain. Instead, she ground her hips in time to his rhythm while grunting softly with every breath.

Danielle arched her back while continuing to ride him. Since she didn't want to push down against his battered torso, she slid her hands through her hair while looking up at the sky. Clint placed his hands upon her breasts, feeling them sway to the motion of her body. When he started to massage them, Danielle placed her hands over his to guide him much as he'd guided her not too long ago.

When she grew anxious, she stopped rocking and started bouncing straight up and down on top of him. That way, she could take every inch of him inside her in a series of powerful thrusts. Clint could feel her climax approaching from the trembling of her muscles to the quickening of her breaths. He pushed her all the way over the edge by pounding into her until she let out a shuddering cry.

Danielle remained perfectly still for a few seconds as her orgasm surged through her from head to toe. Her cheeks were flushed, and her heart was still pounding in her chest when she opened her eyes to look down at him.

"I'm afraid I'm still hurting you," she said.

"Anything but," Clint told her.

"If it's all the same, I think I should finish what I started." As she said those words, she climbed off him and crawled down until her head was once more above his rigid penis. Raking both hands down over his stomach, she wrapped her lips around his cock and sucked him vigorously. Unlike the first time, she wasn't trying to tease or entice him. Danielle knew exactly what Clint needed and she knew exactly how to give it to him. Her tongue pressed against his smooth flesh, and her head bobbed up and down without any sign of letting up.

All Clint could do from there was lie back and enjoy the ride.

SIXTEEN

Although Clint had put on a brave face until being very pleasantly distracted from his injuries, he knew he needed to get some sort of attention if he was going to heal up anytime soon. He still didn't go through the trouble of finding a doctor, since he'd put his body through the wringer more than enough times to tend to himself. Once he and Danielle rode back to town, he visited a barbershop that also advertised hot baths. The pair of dented tubs in the back of the small building on Linden Street weren't much to look at, but the place had everything Clint needed.

The hot water soothed away a good portion of his aches, leaving him with a dull and much more managcable throb in the ribs that had been hit the most. When he stood up to gather his clothes, he did so without letting out a single strained wheeze. After that, he treated himself to a shave as well as a trim.

"Will I see you tomorrow again, Mr. Adams?" the barber asked.

Since he was probably the portly man's best customer in weeks, Clint couldn't blame the barber for not wanting to let him go. "As soon as my whiskers get out of control, this is the first place I'll visit."

The barber smiled. He smiled even wider when Clint tossed him an extra coin on top of what he'd already paid. "I'll be looking forward to it!" he said.

Stepping out of the barbershop, Clint felt like a new man. He strolled down Linden Street, marveling at how many times one path could shift and bend over such relatively flat ground. Despite the lack of boulders, ponds, or any other obstructions, the street took a serpentine shape, as if the men who'd created it never quite decided which direction they wanted it to go. When he reached the spot where Third Avenue branched off from the main route through town, Clint stopped.

Something had been nagging at the back of his mind, and he hadn't quite known what it was. Granted, part of the reason was that he'd been distracted. Danielle was enough to distract any man, but Clint had been forced to deal with plenty more than her since his arrival in Larga Noche. After clearing his head with a ride and a hot bath, among other things, Clint was able to get a handle on what had been bothering him.

The main source of his fretting was Westin himself. Of course, Clint hated steering clear of an asshole like that who'd beaten the tar out of him at gunpoint, but he took comfort in knowing he would be paying Westin a visit real soon. What truly got under his skin was the fact that Westin seemed to be going through a whole lot of trouble to hurt his stepbrother when he could have just as easily beaten Leo to a pulp and taken what he wanted from him. As far as that was concerned, if Westin wanted to hurt Leo some other way, he could have simply put the Dig Dog to a torch.

There was something else behind Westin's actions; possibly someone else, for that matter, causing him to work up such an elaborate trade. As he thought it over some more, Clint found himself walking down Third Avenue. Now that he wasn't looking for a particular place or cursing the idiots who'd put the town together, he saw a lot more than the last times he'd walked that same path.

Instead of a town that had grown outward from some central point like hubs on a wheel, Larga Noche seemed to have been put together in spurts. Small portions of town were separated into even smaller sections to provide stores, entertainments, and services. In another part of town, those same needs were met in another clump of seemingly random buildings. Perhaps someday the town would form larger districts, but there was just as good a chance that Larga Noche would dry up and blow away like so many other settlements before it.

The main reason he thought along those lines was because Clint had been thinking about other people in town who might benefit from what was happening to Leo and his place. The first thing to pop into Clint's mind from there was that other saloons could always do well with less competition. When it came to moving Madeline to another spot, however, that added theaters into the mix. He had yet to see any theaters in Larga Noche, but saloons were a different story. In fact, he'd heard mention of a few other places since he'd been in town.

One of those places was the Tiger's Paw. Just down the street from the Dig Dog was the place marked by an elaborate painting of a tiger. Upon getting a little closer, Clint was able to read the sign that let him know he'd indeed found the place he was after. Preparing himself for the worst, he opened the Tiger's Paw's front door and stepped inside.

Even before he'd been able to soak in everything he was seeing and hearing, Clint knew one thing for certain: If Leo wanted to compete with that place, he was in a whole lot of trouble.

SEVENTEEN

The Tiger's Paw wasn't the largest saloon Clint had ever seen, but it had to be one of the fanciest. The dark blue carpeting on the floor alone could very well have paid for most everything Leo had at the Dig Dog. Even more impressive was the fact that the carpet was the least impressive thing Clint could see.

Apart from the card tables and faro layouts, he spotted other games of chance that he rarely saw outside cities such as San Francisco, Denver, or New York City. As he walked through the place to approach the bar, Clint was greeted by exotic women who looked more like expensive china dolls. One of those was wrapped in dark red silk and had her raven black hair pinned up high so a few long strands could wind over her ears and brush against the ivory contours of her exposed shoulder. She was obviously from the Far East, but he couldn't quite nail down anything more specific than that.

Ruby red lips parted into a smile that was so genuine, Clint thought he might have actually saved the woman's life at one time. "Greetings and welcome to the Tiger's Paw," she said in a rich, melodic voice.

"Hello there," Clint replied. "I was just passing by and thought I could have a look inside." The instant he heard himself speaking to her, Clint wished he could draw the words back into his mouth and never say them again. He hadn't felt so flustered since the first time he'd ever approached a woman.

Bright green eyes reflected the same beautiful smile adorning her face. "You are sweet," she said while taking his arm in a way that felt as if she were melting against him. "Would you like something to drink?"

Almost immediately, Clint regained his composure. "I certainly would, just so long as you have one with me."

Clearly recognizing the change in his demeanor, the Asian beauty leaned against the bar while letting her hand drift all the way down Clint's arm. "I have not seen you here before."

"That's because I'm new in town. I've been spending some time at a place just down the street, though. The Dig Dog. Ever heard of it?"

"I have," she said in a voice that could have said anything at all and made it enticing. "Very strange name."

"It most certainly is."

Offering him her hand, she said, "I am Jade."

"Clint Adams," he replied while taking her hand and kissing it. When he got that small taste of her skin, he couldn't help but wonder what the rest of her tasted like. He tried not to think about it for too long, lest he be too distracted to continue.

"I am glad you've decided to visit the Tiger's Paw," Jade said. "What would you like to drink?"

"What would you recommend?"

"Let me buy you a spiced rum. Just arrived from Boston this week."

"That sounds good." At first, Clint thought he might have

misunderstood the part about her buying the drink for him. The bartender arrived, however, took the order, and handed over two drinks without asking for a cent.

Jade took one of the glasses and raised it. "Here is to good beginnings."

Touching his glass to hers, Clint sampled some of the best rum he'd ever had.

"Do you gamble?" Jade asked.

"Occasionally."

"What do you play?"

"Solitaire mostly."

She smiled again. "I highly doubt that. Why are you here today, Mr. Adams?"

"Why does any man visit a saloon?"

"If you were just any man, you would have made it clear what you wanted by now. I think you have something specific in mind and are just waiting to ask."

Clint took another drink of rum and then set the glass on top of the bar. "Who owns this place?"

"Why do you ask?"

"Because I'd like to buy it."

Jade didn't believe that for a moment. Instead, she smiled at him as she most likely did when any customer told her a bad joke. "Mr. Dhang is a very busy man."

"Mr. Dhang?"

"The owner."

"Fact is, I'd just like to meet the man who put a place like this in the middle of such a backwards town."

Jade's brow furrowed. "Backwards town?"

"Yeah. It seems like whoever put Larga Noche together didn't know whether he was coming or going. After walking the streets for a couple of seconds, I sure as hell didn't."

Compared to the polite smile she'd showed him at his last joke, this one was something completely different. She placed her hand on his arm and let out a laugh that caught the attention of every man within ten feet of where she and Clint were standing. Considering how many people were crammed into that saloon, that was saying something.

"I know just what you mean!" Jade said. "When I first got here, I spent most of my time being lost."

Clint came up with a few humorous stories about their shared frustrations with the town while finishing their rum. When the barkeep took the empty glasses away, Jade wrapped her arm around his and led him toward the gambling tables. "I will take you to see Mr. Dhang."

"Much obliged."

Leaning in to brush against him as she walked, Jade whispered, "I like the way men in this part of the country speak."

"Well, I'm sure I speak for all such men when I say we like the way you do pretty much everything."

Jade laughed again and brushed her hair back, filling Clint's nose with her scent. She escorted him across a room that was filled with almost more people than Clint had seen thus far in the rest of the town. The customers were occupied with all manner of diversions ranging from card games to exotic women. Just when Clint thought they'd reached the edge of the room, Jade took him a bit farther.

Finally, they walked up a narrow set of stairs leading to a floor that was half the size of the main level. It was in the shape of a crescent and built so a good portion of the tables up there could look down on the ones below. The games up there were different than the ones being played on the first floor, as were the players. While the men on the main floor were mostly engrossed in poker or faro, the cards up here weren't even painted with the same symbols or pictures as those. The few tables Clint saw that were using standard decks had the cards spread out in unfamiliar patterns.

The men playing those strange games were dressed in expensive suits that were tailored to fit them perfectly. They all stared at Clint with mild distaste as he passed them by, but were quickly diverted by the woman who was accompanying him. It did Clint some bit of good to know that the men on the second floor were familiar in at least one way.

The table Jade approached was at the farthest point of the floor's crescent shape. It had the best view of the main room and was easily blocked off by a trio of solidly built Asian men whose thickly muscled arms and beefy hands looked as if they'd been molded from granite. Although their suit coats were too well made to give anything away, Clint had no doubts that those men were carrying enough firepower to defeat a small uprising.

There were four men playing whatever game was being hosted at that table. Clint leaned forward to get a look at the cards, but was blocked by a wall of muscle that closed in while scowling at him. One of the men seated at that table wore a suit cut from dark purple silk and frilly cuffs sprouting from both sleeves. At least two of them were Chinese, and the other had a different look to his facial features and body type.

The skinniest of the four men had wrinkled skin that looked as if it had been steamed partially loose from his bones and long wispy silver hair that hung from the back of his scalp and his chin. His clothes weren't as obviously expensive as those worn by the others, and seemed almost as antique as the man wrapped within them. He squinted at Clint, frowned, and said, "Why is this foreigner interrupting us?"

Jade smiled. "His name is—"

"I don't care to hear his name," the old man snapped. Jabbing a finger at the three muscular guards, he said, "Take him from my sight, slit his throat, and leave him outside."

Some of the men chuckled at that, and before Clint could say anything, the old man waggled a bony finger at the closest guard. “No, no,” he said in his screechy voice. “Remove him from my sight, take him outside, and then slit his throat. Better for rug.”

Clint didn’t like that option much better than the first.

EIGHTEEN

Two of the monolithic guards stepped forward while opening their coats to reveal even more guns strapped to them than Clint had anticipated. He knew better than to make a move for his Colt, however, since that would only make a bad situation worse.

"No need for any of this," Clint said. "I'll leave on my own."

Jade tightened her grip on his arm. "He is a guest here," she said in a sharp tone that caused the gunmen to stop in their tracks. "He will be treated as such."

Both gunmen kept their hands within easy reach of their weapons and turned around to look at the card table. The old man there slowly stood up and calmly said, "If he is still here by the time I sit, I will kill him myself." To make his point even clearer, he pulled aside a flap in his jacket and drew a blade that was slender enough to slide between a set of ribs with next to no effort.

Before Clint could finish sifting through the options for escape that would hurt the least, the man next to the Asian fossil reached out with one hand to touch the old man's arm. "That is quite enough," he said in a smooth baritone.

The old man bared his teeth and hissed a string of syllables in a language that didn't quite sound Chinese. The man with the deep voice had a solid build, a round face, and a mustache that didn't have a single whisker out of place. He looked up at the old man and said a few things in the same language that had been spewing from those withered lips.

Still muttering obscenities from another land, the old man sat down.

Rising to his feet, the man who'd put the old man in his place bowed slightly and said, "You will have to excuse him. He is losing quite a lot of money. Mostly due to his poor temperament."

The old man didn't like that one bit and was quite vocal about it.

"Clint Adams," Jade said while gesturing with her free hand, "this is Ki Dhang."

The gentleman with the round face and perfect mustache shook Clint's hand while saying, "I have heard of you, Mr. Adams."

"Have you now?" Clint asked.

"Yes. We are all quite fond of the more colorful stories of this wild land." Glancing down at the old man, Dhang spoke in his native language. The only words Clint recognized in there were his own name. Although the old man's features softened a bit, he was still a long ways from friendly.

"Mr. Adams wanted to have a word with you," Jade said. "I didn't think you would mind."

"Of course not. My friends," Dhang said to the others seated at the table, "excuse me for just a moment."

The other players responded with subtle nods, and their game, whatever it may have been, was quickly resumed.

There was a bar against the back wall that was most likely very well stocked. Clint couldn't tell right away because the bartender was a stunning woman clothed in nothing but a pearl necklace. Her skin was flawless and her proud, ample breasts were only slightly covered by the long black hair that flowed over her shoulders. All Dhang had to do was look at the woman to get her to pour him a drink.

"I will have my usual," Jade said.

"I'll have one of those, too," Clint added.

Before long, two glasses of light green liquor were placed in front of them. Clint picked his up and took a drink. "Absinthe. That's why they call you Jade?"

She smiled, nodded, and drank the liquor as if it were less potent than ice water.

"Mr. Adams," Dhang said while leaning against the bar, "what brings you to my place of business?"

"I've been in town for a short while and thought I'd have a look around. I would've stopped by sooner, but I've had some trouble with a man by the name of Westin Voss."

"I have heard of him. Is he responsible for . . ." Rather than saying the words, Dhang motioned at Clint's bruised face.

"Yeah," Clint said. "Him and some of his friends."

"Most unfortunate. It is dogs like that which give a town a bad name."

"Have you had many dealings with him?"

"I do not allow his kind into the Tiger's Paw." After sipping his drink, Dhang added, "Bad for business."

"So you do know him," Clint said. "Otherwise you wouldn't know what kind he is."

"He did come to see me some time ago. I believe he wanted to force me to pay him protection money. He changed his mind when one of his gunmen disappeared."

Even though he'd barely seen the three hulking gunmen

move, Clint could imagine several different and unpleasant ways those monsters could make someone disappear.

"He is a petty thief," Dhang continued. "Nothing more. I am certain a man of your talents will have no trouble in finding retribution for what was done to you."

"I'm not worried about that. I'm asking around on behalf of Leo Parker."

"Who?"

"He owns the Dig Dog Saloon just down the street."

"Ah yes," Dhang said. "Such an unfortunate name. I have heard that he has a few talented singers working for him." Lifting his glass, he said, "I wish him well."

"Do you know any reason why someone would want to run him out of business?" Clint asked.

"Honestly, Mr. Adams, if you have been inside that establishment, you would know that if a man wanted it to fail, all he would need to do is wait."

For Leo's sake, Clint would have liked to refute that statement. However, he doubted a man who gambled in so many different languages would have gotten far if he couldn't spot a bluff.

"Is there anything I can get for you, Mr. Adams?" Dhang asked. "A seat at one of our high-stakes games perhaps?"

"Perhaps," Clint replied. "For now, though, I'll let you get back to your game before that old man has a fit."

"That old man can arrange three deaths in as many countries with one word," Dhang warned. "You might want to keep your voice down."

"All right, then. I'll just be on my way."

NINETEEN

Clint wasn't exactly thrown out of the Tiger's Paw. He was shown to the door. In his years, he'd been tossed out of plenty of places, and many times the men doing the tossing said they were showing him the door. That usually amounted to his face meeting the door before his body met the street. This time, however, Jade walked with him through the main room and outside, where she parted ways with a kiss on the cheek. When she left him standing outside the saloon, Clint almost thought that leaving had been his idea.

Across the street was another place he intended on visiting. Since he wasn't welcome back inside the Tiger's Paw while that crazy old man was still there, Clint made his way over to a place that had scantly clad women displayed in most of the windows on all three of its floors.

Before Clint had even touched the front door, he'd already been propositioned by at least half a dozen women from the windows as well as the porch. Stepping inside the place should have been a dream come true considering all the ladies that came to meet him. Instead, he felt like a single piece of bloody meat that had been tossed into shark-infested waters.

"Girls, girls, there's only one of me," Clint said.

The woman who got to him first had light brown hair and plenty of curves beneath her light pink dress. The dress's neckline was cut low enough to make Clint wonder how the hell she didn't fall out of it anytime she made a move. She smiled at him with full, red lips and stood so close to him that she was the only thing he could see.

"I'm Kat," she said.

"Hello, Kat."

"Welcome to Miss Tasha's. Come on up to my room and I'll get us both out of all these clothes."

"What is this place?" Clint asked.

She laughed and asked, "You really don't know?"

"No, I know what goes on in here. I mean, is there also a saloon or is it just you girls in here entertaining folks?"

Kat took Clint's arm and led him into the next room. Compared to how Jade had done the same thing at the place across the street, Clint now felt more like he was being dragged. "Funny you should ask. The owner is making some improvements along those lines."

"Really?"

"Yeah. Miss Tasha!" Kat's voice was so loud that anyone within the building could have heard her. Since he was already right beside her, Clint swore his brain rattled between his ears.

The woman who answered the shouted summons reminded Clint of a gypsy fortune-teller who made her living cheating suckers out of their money. Her weathered European features hung on her tired face as though they'd already seen everything the world had to offer and weren't impressed. She wore at least three filmy skirts beneath several belts covered in charms and cheap jewelry that jangled loudly with every step she took.

"Miss Tasha," Kat said to her. "Is the bar open yet? This here fella wants a drink."

"I didn't say that," Clint explained. "I just asked if there was also a saloon in here as well as the other entertainments."

"Other entertainments?" Miss Tasha asked as she reached into a pocket for half a cigar and jammed it into her mouth. "What the hell is that supposed to mean?"

"I think he means us," Kat said.

"He means pussy, he should just say pussy."

"Yeah," Clint said curtly. "That's what I meant."

"Never mind, Miss Tasha," Kat said. "I'll take care of him."

Tasha waved them both off and struck a match against a wall so she could light her cigar.

Kat led him through a parlor and into a larger room that must have taken up a good portion of the entire floor. "Sorry about her," she said. "Miss Tasha's not good with people but she's got a good head for numbers."

"How long has this place been around?" Clint asked.

"Why are you so interested? Most men just come in, pick out what they want, and head to a room upstairs."

"I was just passing by and thought I'd stop in to take a look."

"Some of the girls in the windows draw you in?" Kat asked. "No need to be ashamed. That's what they get paid for."

"And they do a fine job of it." Having gotten a look at the room he was in, Clint could see the makings of a nice little saloon. There was a bar and what looked to be a fairly decent selection of liquor. "What's that over there?" he asked while pointing to a portion of the room that was crammed with pieces of lumber and sectioned off by a tarp.

"Just something that should be built in a while. Look," Kat said. "Do you want a drink?"

"I don't think so."

She reached down to cup his groin. "Do you want something else?"

"Thanks," Clint replied, "but no."

"If you change your mind, I can make you real happy."

Kat's hand worked between Clint's legs with practiced skill that made him stiffen almost immediately.

"I'm sure you could," he said, "but I don't pay for sex."

Abruptly she pulled back her hand, then he was shoved toward the front door and given half a wave as she spun around on the balls of her feet to take the arm of another man, who was allowing his lower regions to make his decisions.

Having had his fill of scouting for a while, Clint headed back to the Dig Dog.

TWENTY

"So," Leo said as he poured Clint a beer, "you basically got kicked out of both places?"

"No." Clint took the beer and had a drink. After a moment, he said, "Well, I guess you could put it that way."

"Sounds like a real successful day of scouting."

"At least someone is bothering to scout. I haven't been in town for very long, and I can already see that your brother has more backing than those two idiots he rides with. If it was just those three, there are several better and quicker ways to cause you misery. He could bust up this saloon from the inside or out. And don't forget the easiest solution of all."

"Don't say it," Leo groaned.

"He could burn this place down."

"I just asked you not to say that."

"Or he or one of his men could just walk right up to you, beat you down, and then put a few bullets into you."

"My brother may hate me," Leo said, "but he wouldn't kill me!"

"He could shoot you without killing you," Clint told him.

"All right. Enough of that. Sorry for what I said about your scouting."

"Apology accepted."

"But if you'd wanted to know more about my neighbors," Leo continued, "I would've been able to tell you just about anything you needed to hear."

"All right, smart ass. Tell me about the Tiger's Paw."

"Mostly a gambling emporium," Leo recited. "Carries plenty of exotic liquors, but not much that the locals would really care to drink. Lots of pretty china dolls working there, and they cook some of the best noodles in New Mexico."

"Noodles?" Clint asked.

Leo nodded and looked in the direction of the Tiger's Paw as if he could see the place through every wall separating them. "Over a dozen varieties. Half of them are original recipes made by the cook that the owner brought in all the way from Sacramento."

"Hmmm. I'll have to see if I can get a taste for myself."

"So you actually found out less than I could have told you. Interesting."

"The owner's name is Ki Dhang," Clint said.

"I knew that."

"He plays host to some powerful men from other states. If I had to wager, I'd say it's just as likely they're from other countries. Even more, I'm fairly certain those men aren't powerful for doing business of the legal variety."

The smug satisfaction disappeared from Leo's face. "You mean criminals?"

"High-ranking ones, I'd say."

"Criminals have a rank?"

"Even outlaw gangs have members that rank higher than others," Clint said. "Some gangs are more like businesses. I've seen a few here and there. There are also outlaws themselves who just wield more power than some brute with a gun or a few followers. I'd say those sorts of men are no strangers to the Tiger's Paw."

Leaning with both elbows on the bar, Leo glanced around as if he was afraid of some demon lurking in a corner somewhere. He didn't have much to worry about in that regard. The only other people to be seen were the usual drinkers and a few more gamblers than normal. On the stage, the guitar player plucked his strings to a new melody while Madeline sang softly to him. "What makes you so sure of all that?" Leo asked.

"I've met powerful men and I've met killers. The men Ki Dhang was hosting were both." After Leo's face had become a pale enough shade of white, Clint added, "Also, there wasn't nearly enough money on that card table to warrant the firepower those men were surrounding themselves with."

The whole truth of it was that Clint was playing a hunch. While his instincts on such matters had saved his life more than once, they weren't exactly gospel. Since playing them off as certainty helped move things along, Clint did just that.

"The good part is that I don't think Ki Dhang or any of his men have anything to do with your problems."

For the first time that day, Leo looked truly hopeful. "Really?"

"Yeah. The Tiger's Paw is doing just fine as it is. He doesn't stand to gain by anything that happens to you. That is, unless you haven't told me something crucial in that regard."

"No. I'm just like you said. Insignificant."

"Great." Seeing all of Leo's hopefulness fade away, Clint added, "Trust me. There are some men who you want to think you're insignificant. Ki Dhang and some of the others he hosts are prime examples."

"You've got me curious. I'd like to meet some of those powerful criminals. Who are they?"

"Smugglers, most likely." Clint couldn't help but be amused when he imagined Leo introducing himself to the crazy old man who'd wanted to slit someone's throat outside to keep his rugs from being stained. "I'm sure Dhang would like to meet his neighbors. Just be sure to bring a gift."

Eventually, Leo straightened up and spoke in a normal tone. "You're pulling my leg right now, right?"

"More or less."

"Speaking of neighbors, I'm sure you found your way to Miss Tasha's."

"Why do you say it like that?" Clint asked.

"Like what?"

"Like some holier-than-thou asshole."

Leo shrugged. "I've done some scouting of my own and heard a few things about you along the way."

"You were checking up on me?"

"When you were just delivering a few bottles, I didn't need to know much where you were concerned. Now that my livelihood and health may be at stake, I'd say it would be smart to know more about everyone involved."

Since that was basically the purpose behind his day of scouting anyway, Clint couldn't really argue with that. "So what did you hear?"

"That you've bedded damn near everything in a dress wherever you go."

"That's a bit much."

"I imagine it's close. I know about you and that gal who runs the stable across town."

Clint shrugged. "All right, but did you get a look at that gal in the stable?"

"Yes I did. Can't say I really blame you there."

"I did get over to Miss Tasha's. Before you say anything else, though," Clint quickly added, "you should know that I don't pay for sex, and I didn't bed any of the girls working there."

"Then that's why it was such a short visit," Leo said. "Unless you're buying opium or time with one of those whores, there's not much reason to be in that place."

"Opium?"

Leo nodded. "That miserable old cow bought her cathouse with profits from opium. She soaks cigars in the stuff and barely bats an eye when one of her customers has so much of it that he never leaves her place alive."

"Sounds like you know quite a lot about that spot," Clint pointed out. "A lot more than you knew about the Tiger's Paw."

"What can I say? Not all of the women working over there are so bad."

"You might change your favorable opinion if you knew that Miss Tasha stands to gain a whole lot by your place being crippled."

"Westin is just after some money," Leo said. "I doubt he wants to cripple me."

"Maybe he doesn't, but a partner of his might not be so charitable."

"And you think Miss Tasha is that partner?"

"It stands to reason. Being set up across from a place like the Tiger's Paw can't be good for her business," Clint explained. "If there's any chance at all that Ki Dhang or any of his associates are involved in the opium trade, that would cut even deeper into her profits."

"Not to mention put her in danger," Leo said. "If what you said about Dhang and his criminal friends is true, that is."

"More than that, I'd say her business may not be doing too well. That's mostly just a gut impression, but it won't take much to see if that's true or not."

Leo's face lit up as he excitedly said, "Of course! A man with your reputation would only be expected to frequent a cathouse."

"Hey! I told you, I don't need to pay any woman to share my bed."

"Of course," Leo said with a wink. "Me neither. If you didn't see anything to make you suspicious, then there are a few more places in town you might want to check."

"You mentioned that Westin wants you to hand over Madeline, right?"

"Yes."

"Well, someone like Miss Tasha could surely put her to work," Clint said.

Leo's muscles tensed and he looked toward the stage as though someone were trying to pull the pretty singer away right in front of him. "Madeline would never work as a whore."

"Sometimes a job like that isn't exactly voluntary," Clint said.

"If that old hag thinks she'll make that dear girl into a slave . . ."

"Actually, even though I don't think that woman is beyond such a thing, I'm not sure that's what she has in mind."

"What, then?" Leo asked.

"Well, it looks like she's turning one of her parlors into something of a saloon."

"Nothing too surprising about that."

"She's building a stage just big enough for a singer or two."

Leo winced. "Uh-oh."

TWENTY-ONE

Clint spent the next day wandering the streets of Larga Noche and looking in on as many saloons or gambling parlors as he could find. None of them stacked up to the Tiger's Paw. In fact, only one of the saloons Clint found was much better than Leo's placc. For the most part, the others were watering holes catering to a few regular customers and their owners weren't interested in doing much more than that.

There was only one other cathouse in the area, and that was a small place about half a mile outside of town. The owner was a stick of a man who was too afraid of Miss Tasha to take one step closer to Larga Noche. A man like that was hardly a threat to anyone else.

After one more day of making the rounds, Clint was convinced that his first instincts were correct and the only other players he needed to be concerned about where Leo's situation was concerned were the owners of the two establishments closest to the Dig Dog. He was also convinced that so much walking didn't do anything to help a set of sore ribs.

After calling it an early night, he made his way back to

the stables to pay Eclipse a visit. The Darley Arabian was just finishing up with a feed bag when Clint approached his stall to give his ear a scratch.

"She taking good care of you, boy?" he asked.

"You know I am," Danielle replied from another stall.

Clint had seen her in there fussing with another horse's hoof, but hadn't said much until now. "Just thought I'd come by and say hello."

"To me or the horse?"

"Both."

After grunting with effort a few times, Danielle replied, "I'm flattered."

"What are you doing over there?"

"This old girl's got a stone under her shoe and I'm just . . ." After one more grunt, she sighed, "There you go! That's better." Her upper body appeared over the stall's gate as she held up a chunk of rock. "Now she'll stop fussing so much," she said while tossing the rock away. "Speaking of fussing, what really brings you by? I know that's a fine horse you've got, but he ain't family."

"I also figured you might be here."

She stepped out of the horse stall and shut the gate behind her. "Go on," she said. As she got closer to him, Danielle reached out to put her hands on him.

Clint smiled. "After our last visit went so well, I thought perhaps—*ow!*"

She'd cut him short by moving her hands directly to his sore ribs and pressing in.

"What the hell?" Clint asked as he backed up a step.

"I was just about to ask you the same thing. What the hell are you doing carousing when you should be resting?"

"Carousing?"

"I have friends in this town other than you, you know," she told him. "I've heard that you've been sticking your nose into every saloon in Larga Noche when you should have been resting."

"That's not the same as carousing," Clint said in his defense. "I've just been having a look around."

She glared at him for a few seconds before sighing, "I suppose I'll believe you."

"No, I think you're going to believe your friends when they told you I wasn't ordering more than one beer in each place."

"And that you didn't let yourself be led away by any of those whores working at them places," she added. "What were you doing in those places, then?"

Clint winced and twisted his body to try and work out a kink in his back. When Danielle saw that, her features softened a bit. "Stay where you are," Clint snapped when he saw her reaching out for him again.

"Don't get squirrelly now," she said as she gently placed her hand on him. "I'm not going to hurt you."

Waiting until she got closer, Clint wrapped his arms around her so he could reach down to cup her backside. "That's a lot better."

Danielle shook her head. "Not now, mister. I'm done tending to one wounded animal, which means I should tend to the next one."

Clint looked around at the other stalls to find Eclipse and one other contented horse apart from the one that had just gotten the stone removed from its shoe. Following her line of sight when he looked back to Danielle, he asked, "You mean me?"

"What other wounded animal do you see? You're coming back to get off your feet so I can wrap them ribs and maybe put something on that busted mess you call a face."

"I suppose that might be a good idea," he admitted as he pushed open the front door and held it for her.

"This is what you had in mind the whole time, isn't it?"

Clint motioned for her to walk ahead of him.

Danielle laughed and shook her head. "You're a real piece of work, Adams."

TWENTY-TWO

It was well past midnight when Leo heard a knock on his office door. He'd been in there for several hours. The first stretch of time had been spent napping on the narrow cot against the wall. He'd been at his desk for the rest of the time, balancing the books and trying not to get too worked up about the totals at the bottom of his ledger pages. There was a fairly good crowd that night. The place was mostly full and had been since early evening. It was always like that when Madeline sang with a guitar and piano player backing her up. As she sang and the musicians played, cards were dealt and liquor was served. And yet, Leo still didn't have much of a reason to join in with the merriment.

Grateful for even a short reprieve, he got up from his chair and opened the door. "Yes?" he said to the older woman standing outside the office.

"You might want to come out here," Henrietta said.

"What is it now?"

"Your brother is here."

"What does he want?" Leo moaned.

"I'm not sure yet. I just thought you should know he was out here with one of those gunmen of his."

"Which one?"

"The man with one arm."

"Aw, Christ," Leo moaned.

"Is any one of them better or worse than the other?" she asked.

"I suppose not."

"Then get out here and have a word with them!"

Wincing as though she could be heard over the commotion in the main room, Leo asked, "What am I supposed to do about them?"

"You know Westin will want to see you," Henrietta said. "And he'll just start some trouble if he doesn't see you quickly enough. Best to head that off and face him right away."

"Fine," Leo griped. "Give me a moment to finish up what I was doing."

Henrietta stuck her head past him to look into the office. When he tried to get in her way, she shoved past him by ducking under his arm. "What were you doing?" she asked.

"Nothing. This is my office, damn it."

"And I'm your partner," she shot back.

"You only own a quarter of this place," Leo pointed out.

"Which means I get at least a quarter of this office."

Knowing he wouldn't be able to get her to leave unless he attempted to toss her over one shoulder, Leo let out an exasperated sigh while running his hands through his unruly red hair. "Why can't you just do what I ask?"

"As soon as you do what I ask," she said. Henrietta pointed to the open ledger on Leo's desk. "You were going through the figures."

"Yes I was. Someone's got to."

"No," she said as she stormed over to the desk and

slammed the ledger shut. "We already know we're in trouble. We're doing all we can to fix it. Agonizing about how deep in the hole we are is only twisting your insides into a knot."

When Leo tried to reach for the ledger, Henrietta snatched it off the desk and tucked it under one arm. Because of her size, the book looked like it was in the hands of a child.

"You want something to do?" she said. "Go out there and face your brother."

"We already know what he wants."

"Then go tell him he can't have it!"

Leo let out a slow breath and nodded. "You're right."

"Of course I am."

"I suppose I'm just a little gun-shy where Westin is concerned."

"That's understandable," she said. "But you can't let a man like that know he's got to you that way. Otherwise, it'll just get worse."

He nodded again. "What would I do without you?"

"Go under quicker than a boat with no bottom," she quickly replied. "Now get out there and show him who's in charge at the Dig Dog."

As Leo left the office, he sighed, "Clint's right. I need to find a new name for this place."

In the space of three steps, Leo had his head held high and his back straight. He patted the young man tending bar on the shoulder and asked, "You selling that new liquor?"

"Yes, sir," the barkeep replied. He was a tall fellow with a face that caught the eye of the women who came through that saloon. More important to Leo, he was also a hard worker and too honest to steal from the till.

"How's it going over?"

"One or two didn't much care for it, but the rest are

liking it just fine. Three men even pooled their money to buy one of the bottles."

"Did they bargain you down on the price?"

The bartender shook his head proudly. "No, sir."

Leo slapped his shoulder one more time, "Good man! Keep it up."

Madeline had just finished up her song, and a good portion of the saloon was applauding. As she took her bows, Leo walked between the tables until he got to one that was near the side of the stage. Two men sat there, each drinking from glasses that had been filled by a bottle they shared. The bottle was half empty and bore the label with a picture of a wolf's head on it.

As soon as he arrived at the table, Leo wished he'd brought the shotgun from beneath the bar. Then again, that would have been a real good way to chase some of his paying customers right into a place where they stood a chance of getting shot. Setting all that aside, he leaned down so he could be heard over the noise in the saloon and said, "I'm going to have to ask you to leave, Westin."

"But I ain't doing nothing," Westin said.

"After what you did the last time, you're not welcome here. Now get on out of here or I'll have to escort you myself."

Westin turned to the man beside him and smirked. "Well now, Samuel. Look who grew a pair of balls in the last couple of days."

"Impressive," the one-armed man said.

"Come on," Leo announced. "Let's go."

TWENTY-THREE

Leo led the way outside. Although he managed to keep himself fairly steady and his stride at a constant pace, he was fighting back a nasty bout of the shakes. Every step of the way, he expected to feel either a clubbing blow to the back of his head, a punch to the kidneys, or a bullet through his spine. He'd weathered plenty of the first two throughout his years growing up with Westin. He never would have seriously expected the third option until the last few days.

When he rounded the corner of his building, Leo took a step into an alleyway. He stopped short of ducking completely into the shadows, however, in hopes that the number of people walking up and down the street would keep things relatively civil.

"You've made your point, Westin," Leo said as he spun around to face the other two men. "I'm trying to pull together what you asked."

"I don't think you are," Westin replied. He stepped up to stand so close to Leo that he forced the other man to put his back against the closest wall. "If you were, that pretty lady in there would be introducing herself to me. Instead, she barely knows who I am."

"I'm talking about the money. That's what I'm trying to get."

"We don't want the money anymore," Samuel said. The one-armed man's voice was like a set of rusty nails gouging into Leo's ears.

"Then . . . what do you want?" Leo asked.

When Westin grabbed hold of him by the collar and slammed him up against the wall, it was a welcome reminder of days gone by for Leo. At least it gave him something else to think about instead of the killer gazing at him. "You know what we want, you damn fool," Westin snarled. "We want you to tell that songbird in there that she's going with us."

"Why do you even need me to do that?" Leo asked. "I mean, what do you expect me to do? I don't even have a signed agreement with her. She's free to come and go as she pleases."

"So you'll just introduce us and step aside," Samuel said.

Leo regretted saying anything to the men in front of him. He regretted bringing them outside and far away from so many witnesses. The street was disturbingly empty at the moment, and all he could think about were accounts of men who'd been gunned down in the middle of the night when nobody lifted a finger to stop the killers.

Doing his best not to let his fear show too much, Leo said, "Madeline is a singer. That's all."

Samuel nodded. Clearly, he didn't give a damn about what was being said.

Shifting his eyes to his stepbrother, Leo continued, "If you want her to sing, make her an offer."

"What she does after she leaves this shit hole," Samuel said as he stepped forward to push Westin aside like so much trash, "don't concern you. All you need to worry about is agreeing to whatever story that comes your way just so long as it ends with her being contracted to us."

"But I already told you, and I told Westin, that me and Madeline don't have a contract!"

"Then write one up, date it for whenever she first got here, and make her sign it," Samuel said. "Anyone comes along, lawmen or such, family, you tell them that the first contract was legal and so was the second."

"But that won't hold up forever. Just let me get the money together to pay you," Leo said. "This is insane."

"Are you calling me crazy?" Samuel asked in a voice that chilled Leo to the bone.

When he looked over at his stepbrother, it was the first time Leo was absolutely certain that Westin wasn't the one in charge. "No," Leo said. "Of course not. I'm just saying that I can make a lot more profits if Madeline stays where she's at. I've got some other plans in mind that will turn things around for the Dog real quick. Name your price and I'll pay it. More than you asked before!"

"Other plans, huh?" Samuel grunted. "You mean like that piss water you're selling like it's gold in a bottle? What's that supposed to get you?"

"A reputation," Leo said. "Fancy liquor can turn a saloon into a respected establishment attracting fancy customers. When word spreads that folks can drink spirits here that they can't get hardly anywhere else, it'll bring in some curious men with deep pockets. Word will also spread about the beautiful girl singing her heart out. Men who come for one will see the other, and before you know it, all them good words are spreading like wildfire."

Leo's eyes bounced back and forth between the two men in front of him as the words kept spilling from his mouth. Although a few more locals were walking down the boardwalk past them, they either didn't care about what was happening or knew it was often healthier to leave well enough alone.

"And the thing is," Leo continued, "there doesn't need to be many rich men like that coming around. Just a few because I'm also working to get the Dog on the gamblers' circuit. Once some of those card players come by and see the money that can be made at one of my tables, they'll bring more gamblers around for a taste."

Westin's eyebrows rose. "Rich men like to gamble and a few of them can drop a good amount of cash at a few games."

"That's right!" Leo said. "When they're sick of gambling, they'll drink, and while they're drinking, they'll enjoy Madeline's singing. When they leave, they talk about what a good time they had here, and it starts all over again. In the meantime, I'll be building up the Dog into the best saloon in New Mexico."

"And while you're doing all of this, you'll be giving me and my boys a cut of whatever you earn," Westin reminded him.

"Naturally."

Westin looked to Samuel and said, "That seems like a good way to go. Even if he's not able to pay up, we can still take whatever we like."

"We'll take it anyway," Samuel said. "And since it took this long to come up with the money, we're setting down another plan. You're going to start a new business in this place, and just so you don't think we're heartless, you'll be allowed to keep a small percentage of the profits for yourself."

"What about Madeline?" Leo asked.

"She's still coming with us. You'll also put some other girls on your payroll under a contract that I'll bring to you tomorrow. They'll be singing, serving drinks, cleaning up, whatever the hell you want to tell them. Soon as they get here, you hand them over to us."

"What for?"

"That doesn't matter," Samuel replied. "You just do what you're told, and in exchange for that, after a year, you'll be rid of us to run your business however you like. You'll also have a nice little nest egg to follow through on whatever idiotic plans you come up with between now and then."

"Sounds like a fair trade," Westin said. "Maybe you should take it."

"It sounds like you want to turn me into someone like the two of you," Leo said in disgust. "I won't have any part of that."

"Maybe you're right," Samuel told him. "Maybe we do want to turn you into someone like us. Westin, hold his hand up against that wall."

Westin glared sternly back at him and said, "He's got the message. This don't need to go any farther."

"Do what I told you. Now."

Reluctantly, Westin grabbed Leo's left wrist.

"Not that one," Samuel said. "The other hand."

Leo struggled, but couldn't get past the two men who'd formed a wall directly in front of him. When he tried to force his way between them, he was roughly shoved back. Leo tried once more to get away, but his right wrist was already locked in a tight grip and Westin's other hand had clamped around his throat to shove him back again.

Pinning Leo to the wall with just as much ease as he'd pinned him to the ground during all of their childhood fights, Westin looked his stepbrother in the eyes and said, "Sorry about this, Leo."

When Leo looked back at Samuel, he saw a flicker of motion as the gunman's left arm crossed his body to snatch the pistol from its holster. There was a shot that sent a ringing through his ears and a sharp bite of pain from his hand. Leo's eyes darted to that hand to find his middle finger had been blown off.

Without a word, Samuel squeezed his trigger again to turn the next finger on Leo's hand into red pulp. He thumbed back the hammer, paused, and said, "Do what we ask or things'll get a lot worse." He then holstered the pistol as he and Westin walked away.

TWENTY-FOUR

The following morning, Clint strode up Sharp Bend along a route that had become all too familiar. When he arrived at his destination, however, he stopped and stared at the saloon's front window for a good long while. The lettering painted upon the glass was blacked out and two boys in their teens worked to hang a sign from a post near the door. One of the boys was handing the sign up to the other, who stood precariously atop a ladder. Since he couldn't decide which one was about to get hurt first, Clint rushed over to the closer young man. He made it just as the sign began to slip from his grasp.

"Thanks, mister," the teen said. "I been holding that up there all damn day."

The boy on top of the ladder replied, "That's only because you wouldn't help me get these hooks where they were supposed to be!"

"It ain't a two-man job!"

"Now it's a three-man job," Clint said. "How about we just get it done?"

Both of the boys looked at him and nodded. "Yes, sir," replied the one on the ladder.

As they worked to get a few hooks embedded into the post protruding from the saloon's front wall and hang the sign, Clint asked, "Whose idea was this?"

"Miss Henrietta's," said the kid helping Clint to lift the sign. "She sent us out to pick up the sign and then hang it. Paying us a dollar to do it, too."

"That's . . . fifty cents each," corrected the boy on the ladder.

"Right. Like I'd cheat my own brother."

Clint winced as he thought about the bad blood flowing between brothers at that particular saloon, but kept his thoughts to himself. The sign was wrapped in burlap, which made it slippery to handle. "It would sure be easier if we took off this cover," he said.

"No!" both teens said in unison. As the one up top guided the rings on the sign's upper edge into the hooks in the post, the other one explained, "She wanted to keep it covered."

"For how long?" Clint asked.

"Until you got here," Henrietta said from just behind the batwing doors. Placing a hand on each door, she pushed them open while stepping outside. She looked up at the sign, which loomed well over the top of her head. Making up for her short stature with a strong flick of her wrist, she tossed a fifty-cent piece up to the boy on top of the ladder. "You've done a great job." Shifting a critical gaze toward the closer of the two boys, she added, "And it only took you twice as long as I thought it would."

Once again, the boys spoke in unison when they pointed to each other and said, "It's his fault!"

"You can both thank your lucky stars that Mr. Adams arrived later than I expected as well," she said. "Are you about finished here?"

"Yes, ma'am," said the boy standing beside Clint.

Henrietta clapped her hands together. "Excellent! It's time for the unveiling. I'm sure you'll enjoy this, Clint."

"I can barely wait," he said.

After getting a nod from Henrietta, the boy at the top of the ladder pulled off the burlap that had been covering the sign.

"The Howling Hound?" Clint asked as he read the flowing letters. Those words framed a black drawing resembling the wolf's head on the label of the liquor that had brought him to Larga Noche in the first place. "Does Leo have a fondness for dogs?"

"Yes, indeed. At least this dog has stopped digging and is setting its sights higher."

After taking a moment to study it, Clint nodded. "I like it."

"As do I." Leaning in and nudging him with her elbow, Henrietta added, "And it beats the hell out of the other terrible names Leo came up with."

"Can we go now?" the boy on the ladder asked.

"Absolutely."

The boy next to Clint spoke up as well. Handing over his fifty-cent piece, he asked, "Can I have some of that fancy liquor I heard about?"

"You can't afford it," she said, "but please spread the word."

Clearly disappointed, the boy tightened his fist around his coin and started walking down the street. His brother jumped down from the ladder so both of them could cross Sharp Bend and run straight toward Miss Tasha's.

"Boys will be boys," Clint said.

"And men will be late. Especially," Henrietta said, "men connected to this saloon."

"Why do you say that?" Clint asked.

"Because Leo hasn't shown up today."

"What?"

Her face darkened. "He stood up to his brother last night, and now he's at his house, Clint. You should go and see him."

Judging by the look in her eyes, it wasn't going to be a pleasant visit.

TWENTY-FIVE

Getting directions to Leo's home near the outskirts of town wasn't difficult. Following them, on the other hand, was a challenge. Clint may have had an easier time if Leo had lived just outside of town so he could leave Larga Noche's boundaries and circle in from there. Since that wasn't the case, he had to navigate the infuriating tangle of streets until he found the house he was after.

Clint's knuckles pounded on the door hard enough to rattle it in its frame. When the door was opened, Leo scowled out at him while saying, "Easy! If you intended on knocking the damn thing down, you would have at least saved me the trouble of getting up!"

"Henrietta told me you stood up to Westin last night," Clint said as he immediately looked down at Leo's bandaged hand. "I take it that didn't go well."

Leo stepped aside so Clint could enter, and then he shut the door. His house was barely larger than a cabin. Most of the entryway was taken up by a hat rack and a set of stairs leading to the second floor. Straight ahead was a kitchen and small table while to the right of the front door was a parlor with a fireplace, a rocker, and a small table with a few books stacked upon it.

Making his way to the rocker, Leo sat down with a labored grunt. "What did she tell you?" he asked.

"Just that Westin and one of his men came along last night and she asked you to show them the door. You had a word with them and the three of you took it outside."

"That's it?"

"She said she thought she heard gunshots."

"Yeah," Leo said. "That's the part where it would have been nice to have a little backup."

"I'm sorry. I should've been there."

"You're doing enough. Henrietta may be small, but she knows how to handle that shotgun I keep below the bar."

"She wasn't even certain she'd heard the shots," Clint explained. "She told me as much. She also told me she went outside to look for you when you didn't come back in and she found you passed out lying against a wall."

Leo stared down at the flickering light in his fireplace. "When I woke up, I was in my own bed with the doctor looking down at me. I thought I was dead."

"Something tells me you wouldn't have needed a doctor if that was the case," Clint said.

"Well, I wasn't thinking too straight at the time. I didn't even think about how I got here."

"Henrietta found you, gathered whoever she could, and brought you back here. She sends her best, by the way."

"She's a good woman. I'm glad she didn't try to come out when Westin and that one-armed son of a bitch did this to me."

Clint looked down at Leo's hand. "If you don't mind me asking, what did they do to you?"

"See for yourself," Leo said as he unwrapped enough of

the bandages for Clint to see the bloody little nubs where the two middle fingers of his right hand had been.

Clint pulled in a sharp breath. "Damn! What the hell was that for?"

"They was proving a point." Leo wrapped up his hand again and set in gingerly across his lap. "I knew my brother had a mean streak and that he didn't care for me too much, but I never thought he'd go so far as to maim me this way."

"It could have been a lot worse," Clint said.

"What's that supposed to mean?"

"It means they could have killed you. Why didn't they?"

"How the hell am I supposed to know?"

Clint walked to the kitchen to get them both some water. The house was small enough that he didn't have to raise his voice very much to be heard in the next room when he said, "I heard of a gunman out in Nebraska, I think, who got his hand hurt a lot worse than that. He needed a special gun made, but he was back out and raising hell before too long."

"What happened to him?" Leo asked.

Walking into the parlor carrying two cups of water, Clint told him, "I'm not sure. I'll have to ask around next time I'm out that way. All we need to worry about for the moment, though, is what happens to you. Where do you go from here, Leo?"

"Hell if I know," he sighed.

"Why don't you start by telling me what happened last night."

After taking a sip of water, Leo steeled himself and then began speaking in a steady voice to describe what happened the last time he'd seen his stepbrother. Every so often, his voice wavered but another deep breath and drink of cool water put him back on track. "When the first shot was fired," he said, "I thought I was dead. The second one came and I don't recall much from there."

"Understandable," Clint said. "Must've hurt like a bastard."

"Still does."

"So they want you to piece together some sort of contract so you can legally hand over Madeline?"

"That's right," Leo said. "Most likely, I'd say she's going to be the first girl in a long line. If I hand her over, there'll just be more."

"You mentioned something about another business they wanted to start?" Clint asked.

Leo nodded. "Opium."

"They want to turn your saloon into an opium den?"

"No. They want to sell opium and some other things like that from my place. They also want to use my saloon to store boxes while they're being shipped across the country. Kind of like a depot."

"Could be guns," Clint said. "Or stolen property."

"Or any number of illegal things," Leo said as he jumped to his feet. "Otherwise, they could just ship the damn things like normal folks! What gets under my skin is what they want to do to Madeline and the other girls they intend on bringing to my place. I can't even imagine . . ."

Clint could imagine it just fine. Doing so lit a fire deep in his gullet. "They're scared," he said.

"Funny," Leo replied as he held up his bandaged hand, "they didn't seem that way to me."

"They're nervous about something, which is why they've stepped up their game."

"I still doubt they're scared of anything."

Clint grinned. "Then we'll just have to see what we can do to remedy that."

TWENTY-SIX

It hadn't taken much to find someone who recognized Clint's description of Westin's men. In fact, one of the first people he'd asked was the desk clerk at the hotel where he was staying. Clint had just been finishing breakfast when he'd noticed the front desk of his hotel faced a window that looked directly out to Linden Street.

"I don't know about any one-armed man," the clerk had told him, "but that big bald fellow sounds familiar. He spends a lot of time at Mackie's."

Mackie's was another one of Larga Noche's saloons. Clint had been there a handful of times when he'd been scouting such places in town. Also, it was just down the street from his hotel so he'd stopped in there for a drink when he wasn't of a mind to go all the way to Leo's place.

"When was the last time he was there?" Clint asked.

"He's there every morning for biscuits and gravy."

"You know what he eats?"

The clerk shrugged. "Lots of folks go there for biscuits and gravy. Mackie's serves 'em up almost every morning.

They taste like bricks and mortar, but they're cheap and there's always plenty of them."

Clint had figured someone like Westin and those other two couldn't be too hard to miss in a town the size of Larga Noche, but he thought he'd have to look a bit harder than that. Without questioning his bit of good luck, he thanked the clerk and headed out the door.

Thanks to the rest he'd had over the last day or two, Clint was able to move without feeling a stabbing jolt of pain from his ribs. What hurt even more was the jab he felt to his pride whenever he thought about how his ribs had gotten that sore in the first place. He felt a whole lot better once he caught sight of Kurt sitting at a table in the little saloon down the street.

Mackie's was half the size of Leo's place. Its main room contained only a bar and seven tables situated near a stage that was just big enough to hold three dancing girls as long as they didn't move around very much. At the moment, the only thing on that stage was a table stacked high with breakfast so the few paying customers there could help themselves. Since there was only one door in or out of the main room, Clint picked a spot across the street where he could wait without being easily seen.

Before too long, Kurt stepped outside wearing a big smile on his face and gravy stains on the front of his shirt. He didn't cast a second glance in Clint's direction before heading up Linden Street and turning onto Third Avenue.

By this time, Clint could have walked to Larga Noche's largest collection of saloons in his sleep. He had no trouble whatsoever following Kurt through town all the way to Sharp Bend. When the big bald man drew closer to Leo's place, Clint rested his hand upon his holstered Colt in anticipation of putting it to use. Instead of barging in to pay Leo a visit, Kurt took a few moments to gaze up at the new sign before moving along.

Kurt's next stop was Miss Tasha's. When he got there, he did a lot more than just look at the sign over the door. He stepped up onto the porch and was immediately greeted by a dark-haired girl wearing a slip of a dress with a neckline that was cut low enough to expose a generous portion of her small breasts. She went to work on him right away by rubbing his chest and pressing herself against him. Although Clint couldn't hear what the two of them were saying, Kurt's leering smile was easy enough to read from afar. It seemed the two of them had just about bartered an agreeable price as Clint crossed the street and prepared to step inside the cathouse in Kurt's wake. With any luck, he'd be able to talk to one of the girls long enough for Kurt to get nice and comfortable in his room before Clint cut his visit short.

As Clint opened the door, he could see Kurt inside being led upstairs by the skinny girl who'd set her sights on him. Even closer, however, was a young man with a very familiar face. That young man recognized Clint right away and ruined Clint's hopes of following Kurt unseen when he said, "Mr. Adams!"

Just past the young man, Kurt stopped on the stairs and began turning around.

TWENTY-SEVEN

Clint reached out to grab the front of the boy's shirt and pull him outside with the same speed he would use to draw his Colt. Like many of the men who'd found themselves on the wrong end of that Colt, the boy who'd been on his way out of the cathouse gaped in surprise and struggled to catch his next breath.

After dragging the kid outside, Clint kept moving until he could duck around a corner and throw the boy against a wall. When the young man tried to speak again, Clint slapped his hand against the boy's mouth. The teenage boy stared at him with wide, petrified eyes without making another move.

Around the corner, Clint could hear the front door open and a few heavy footsteps knock against Miss Tasha's front porch. A pair of working girls were sitting out there, but they knew better than to get involved with other folks' business.

The door creaked open again and a woman said, "What are you doing, sweetie? Come back inside."

"Who was just out here?" Kurt asked.

When he heard Kurt's voice, Clint reflexively pressed his hand tighter against the young man's face. Now that he'd had a moment to think, he recognized the boy as one of the teens who'd helped hang the new sign in front of Leo's saloon. When he wasn't on top of a ladder, the boy turned out to be a bit shorter than Clint had guessed.

"You," Kurt grunted. "Who just walked through that door?"

One of the women on the porch answered the question in a slow, lazy voice. "Wasn't that just you?"

"Before me, you stupid bitch!"

"I guess there were some men walking out," she said. "Imagine that. Men leaving a place like this."

One heavy boot thumped against the porch. Even though he couldn't see anyone on there from his spot around the corner, Clint could hear a definite shift in the woman's voice when she said, "Take one more step and I'll start screaming. Then Armand will come out to check on me."

Whoever Armand was, Kurt must not have wanted to draw his attention, because the next sound Clint heard was the creak of the front door again. "So you didn't see anyone?" Kurt asked.

"Just the sweet little thing that was with Sally."

Clint glanced over at the young man in front of him and felt a smirk form beneath his restrictive hand.

After a few seconds, the dark-haired woman with Kurt purred something to him and the door was shut. Clint waited for a spell before risking a quick look around the corner. Miss Tasha's front porch was once again occupied by just the two working girls who rested there. The closest lady saw Clint right away and gave him a nod.

Taking his hand away from the young man's face, Clint pushed him farther down the alleyway. "What's your name?" he asked.

"W-Will."

"First of all, I apologize for dragging you out here like this."

"Did I do something wrong?"

"Not at all," Clint said. "You know that man who was walking in right ahead of me?"

"Yes. He's one of the men that comes to the Dig Dog sometimes. Or . . . I mean the Howling Hound."

"Right. Have you seen him very much?"

"Not really, but I know he's not the sort of man I'd like to see very often."

Clint smiled. "You're a smart kid, Will." Seeing the twitch on Will's face, Clint added, "Sorry. Not a kid. Do you frequent this place very often?"

Will shrugged as if he'd been caught at something. "I come around every now and then to talk to the ladies. I been saving up for . . . well . . . you know."

"Sure I do. And that bit of money that Miss Henrietta gave you put you over the top."

"That's right. Since it was my first time . . ." Will stopped himself and flushed in the cheeks.

"We all have a first time, Will," Clint said as he took a look around. So far, nobody was taking much of an interest in their conversation. "Nothing to be ashamed of. Did she take care of you?"

"Oh yeah," Will said through a grin that stretched nearly every muscle in his face. "Twice. She even let me sleep there and gave me a bath in the morning."

It sounded to Clint like she'd overcharged him and then decided to make up for it. Still, he doubted any young man would be too angry about such a thing. That didn't happen until his fifth or sixth time.

"Sounds like a hell of a deal," Clint said. "I've got another deal for you."

Will scowled and recoiled a bit as he looked Clint up and down.

"Not that kind of deal!" Clint said. "I've got a job for you to earn some extra money. Might not be enough for another all-night party, but it should get you back in one of those ladies' good graces."

"I'm just interested in one of them," Will sighed.

"Of course you are." Clint dug some money from his pocket and slapped it against Will's chest. "Here's half up front. I want you to go back in there and see if you can find out what that fellow is up to. The bald one. I'd go in, but he'd recognize me."

"That's why you didn't want me to say your name when he was right there!"

"Smart lad. See if you can find out where he is in there and who he's with. Ask the girls, not anyone else. They're used to keeping secrets, and we don't need this one kept for more than a few minutes. If you have to, slip one of them a bit of this money and they'll give you something at least."

"What if I can find out more?" Will asked.

"Then you'll get more when you come back. Just watch yourself. That man's a killer, so don't get too close."

"Okay. I'll just ask around."

"I'm not kidding here. Being stupid will only force me into something I want to avoid," he explained while patting the gun on his hip. "If you get nervous or if he seems suspicious, come right back out here and find me. Got it?"

"Yeah."

Since Will seemed nervous enough to be cautious but not jittery, Clint sent him on his way.

TWENTY-EIGHT

Will had been gone for less than a minute when Clint stepped back around the corner and onto the porch in front of Miss Tasha's. Both ladies who'd been out there before were still there now. One of them, a slender blonde in her twenties, sat in a chair with one leg draped over the arm in a way that caused her skirts to fall away just enough to present an interesting view to passers-by.

"Howdy," she said. "Thought you were gonna hide in the alley all day long."

"The view on this side of the building is a whole lot better," Clint said. He took a bit of money from his pocket and offered it to her. "This is for before," he said. "For when that bald fellow was asking about me."

She took the money, folded it up, and slid it down the front of her body. After tugging the front of her dress down to expose one dark little nipple, she eased her clothing back into place and put the money into a pocket. "Yeah," she said. "I thought you'd appreciate that. I don't care much for that one anyway."

"Really? Why not?"

"He comes along like he owns the place. Like he owns us. He's rough when he's with us. He likes to throw us around when he takes us upstairs."

Clint looked over to the other girl. She was younger and had a little more meat on her bones, which made her very easy on the eyes. The troubled expression on her face when the subject of Kurt had been brought up wasn't so pretty.

"Does he prefer any one of you over the other?" Clint asked.

Both women shook their heads.

"What about today? Do you know what he's doing in there today?"

"I don't care," said the younger girl. "Just so long as he's not doing it with me."

"Why all the questions?" the other woman asked. "He owe you money or something?"

"It's more than that," Clint said. "Any way you could find out some more about him or any of the men he might run with?"

"Maybe," the blonde said. "But it'll cost more."

"Why?"

"Because they're dangerous."

Clint stepped a little closer to the blonde with her leg hiked up on the arm of her chair. "Sounds like you already know a thing or two on the matter."

"Could be."

Digging into his pocket, Clint discovered he was almost out of cash. Leaving just enough to have something for Will when he came out, he took out one bill and discreetly gave it to her. "What's your name?" he asked.

The blonde took the money in an experienced hand, only to make it disappear quicker than if she were showing him a magic trick. "Ingrid," she told him.

"Will you have something to tell me later tonight?"

"I can tell you a thing or two right now if you like."

He shook his head. "It'll have to be later. How about seven o'clock?"

"You come back here and I'll be waiting," Ingrid said.

"If I can't make it, can you come to me?"

"Where?"

"There's a hotel all the way down on Linden."

"The place near Mackie's?" she asked.

"That's the one. Come by there if I don't show up here. Is that all right?"

She looked Clint over and seemed to like what she saw. "For you, sure."

Just then, the front door swung open and Will stepped outside. He wore an excited look on his face and could barely contain himself once he spotted Clint. "Mr. Adams, I—"

Clint grabbed him by the arm and dragged him away from the front of the cathouse. As soon as they picked a spot in front of the neighboring store, Will said, "Sorry about that, but that fella you wanted to know about isn't in a spot where he can hear me."

"You're sure about that?"

"Oh, yes. He's busy with one of the girls inside. They just went up to her room."

"Do you know which room?" Clint asked.

Will nodded. "The end of the hall on the right. I even got a key."

When Clint saw the key in Will's hand, he could hardly believe it. "Why the hell did you get a key?" he asked.

"I thought you might want it. Don't you want to go and see him? Isn't that why you wanted to know all of this? Anyway, my mother always says it's better to have more and not need it than not have enough."

Clint took the key from him. "Smart lady. You're sure this is the right one?"

"Yeah. I did what you said and asked the girls. Actually, I just needed to ask one, and since she was the same one who was with me, I didn't need to pay her any more. She said none of the girls really likes that man or any of the others that have been coming around here."

"How many others?"

"She didn't say," Will replied. "But she did say that the fella you're after is kind of quick. Whatever that means."

"All right, then," Clint said as he handed Will the rest of his payment. "I won't waste any more time."

TWENTY-NINE

Clint walked through the cathouse with purpose. Some of the women who weren't with customers watched him, but they knew when a man should be approached and when he should be left alone. One of them knew Clint a bit better than the rest, and she approached him straight away. Rather than trying to discourage her or steer her in another direction, Clint smiled broadly and wrapped an arm around the buxom redhead.

"Back for more?" she asked. "I knew you wanted something other than a tour of our parlor."

"You are very right," Clint said without breaking stride. "And that's why I came back. I don't believe I caught your name last time."

"You never asked for it."

"I'm asking now."

"Why do you want it now?" she asked. "You're not interested in fucking."

"How do you know?"

"Because you haven't done one thing to make me think you were. Why are you here, Clint?"

They were at the foot of the stairs leading up to the rooms where most of the working girls conducted their business. The redhead had a firm grip on Clint's arm and wasn't about to let go anytime soon. He turned to her and said, "This is as far as I need you to go. Just do yourself a favor and stay away from here for a spell."

"Why? Are you going up to look in on Kurt?"

"Why do you ask?"

"Because that sweet boy who was in here before asked about him and bolted from here like his tail feathers were about to be plucked. Now you show up."

"All right," Clint said. "Would it be a problem if I did need to have a word with Kurt?"

"No."

"And if those words got a bit loud?"

She smirked. "Make that asshole squeal as loud as you can. Ain't none of us girls going to lift a finger to stop that. You might have a bit of trouble from Miss Tasha, though." She let go of Clint's arm and rubbed his chin. "Don't worry about it none," she said. "I'll keep this area as clear as I can for as long as I can. Just try not to shoot anyone other than him."

She said that last part with a wink, and Clint allowed her to think that was a joke as he went upstairs and headed for the right-hand door at the end of the hall. Once he was there, Clint took a moment to wonder just how much he was going to trust a kid who he barely knew. He eased the key into the lock, turned it, and felt no resistance whatsoever. Putting his shoulder to the door, he eased it open as quietly as he could. As it turned out, he didn't need to be quite so cautious since the people in that room were more than a little preoccupied.

"Get on your knees," Kurt said from his spot near the bed. He stood with his back to the door, naked as the day he was born and looming over a young girl dressed in nothing but an unbuttoned blouse.

Clint opened the door slowly, resisting the urge to hurry inside before Kurt could touch the young woman again. Once he got a bit closer, Clint saw that he was already too late on that account. The girl crawled off the bed and did as she was told. As soon as she was kneeling, Kurt took a firm grip of her hair with one hand.

A split second after the girl had caught sight of Clint entering the room, Kurt wrenched her head in the other direction while snarling, "Look at me, bitch."

Although he couldn't see exactly how excited Kurt was at that moment, Clint could read what he needed in the other man's voice. When the girl attempted to pull away from him, Kurt brought up his other hand, which was wielding a hunting knife as he gripped the woman's hair with enough force to pull it from its roots.

"You know what I want, you damn whore," Kurt said. "Now give it to me before—"

The barrel of Clint's Colt tapped against the back of Kurt's head, freezing him in his spot. "How about we take a moment to think about what the lady wants," Clint said. "From where I'm standing, I'd guess she wants to get the hell out of this room. Am I right?"

"Y-Yes," she replied.

"Let her go," Clint demanded.

Remaining rooted to his spot without moving a muscle, Kurt said, "There's money on the dresser. Take it."

"I'm not robbing you. Let her go. Now."

Kurt released his grip on the girl's hair, allowing her to scurry away on all fours like a frightened rabbit.

"Collect your clothes and get out," Clint told her.

She hurried to gather her clothes and was out of the room before anyone had a chance to say another word. After the door shut, Clint said, "Drop the knife."

Kurt held his ground and didn't relax his grip on the hunting knife. "That voice sounds familiar."

"It should."

Without any regard for the precarious position he was in, Kurt turned around to look over his shoulder at the man behind him. "Oh yeah," he said through a wide smile. "I kicked the hell out of you not too long ago. Your face is looking better. How are them ribs?"

"Better. How about you tell me why you're here."

"If you don't know why I'm here, I must've hit you harder than I thought."

"No. I mean why you're here in a shit hole town like this one when there are much greener pastures not too far away. You and Westin are into a lot more than wringing money from saloon keepers, right?" When he didn't get an answer, Clint thumbed back the Colt's hammer and tapped the end of the barrel once more against Kurt's head. "Right?"

"Yeah, yeah," Kurt spat. "Right."

"So tell me more about that."

"The best I can tell you is to leave this room, leave this town, and do both of them things real quick."

"So there truly is something good brewing around here," Clint mused. "I know you're not exactly paid to think, but try to recall as much as you can about the business you and Westin are involved in. While you're at it, tell me just who the hell that one-armed asshole is who rides with you. You can use short words if that makes it easier."

Kurt met Clint's eyes and said, "Real tough talk from the man with the gun. This would be a whole lot different if things were leveled out."

"You want level, huh?" Clint said as he holstered the Colt. "I was hoping you'd say something along those lines."

THIRTY

Marching Kurt down the hall and up the next flight of stairs was arguably one of the best times Clint had ever had inside a cathouse. His conversation with the big bald man hadn't taken long. Since Clint wasn't outnumbered three to one and being held at gunpoint, the conversation went a whole lot better than the last one he'd had with Kurt. Sure, Clint was sporting a few fresh bruises and one small cut on his temple, but Kurt looked like he'd been run over by a locomotive.

All of the fight was out of the big fellow, and he stumbled with every other step. Whenever he faltered too much, Clint shoved him forward and grunted, "Keep moving." There wasn't even a need for Clint to have his pistol drawn. Judging by the dazed expression on Kurt's face, he barely knew what was going on. He was so confused, in fact, that he didn't realize he was still naked.

After making it to the third floor amid a flurry of whispers and giggles from the girls they passed along the way, Clint slapped him on the cheek to wake him up a bit. "That room there," he said while pointing to the door at the end of the hall. "That's the one you told me about?"

"Yeah," Kurt groaned.

"That's the one where he is?"

"Yeah."

"Is he in there now?" When he didn't get an immediate reply, Clint grabbed Kurt's face and shook him hard enough to hurt. "Don't lie to me! You make one wrong move now and I'll beat you worse than I did before."

Finally, a spark showed in Kurt's eyes as he wheeled around to face Clint. He still couldn't hide the twitches of pain from all the fresh welts and cuts coming from the fight he'd recently lost. "I ain't lying!" he fumed. "He's in there. He's always in there except for when he goes out to gamble and that ain't until later at night. Every goddamn night!"

Clint nodded. "All right. I believe you."

"Good. Are we done?"

"There's just one more thing for you to do before we're done."

With that, Clint grabbed Kurt by one shoulder and the back of his neck. On any other day, the big man would have been able to pull free from that. But after the punishment Clint had given him in his room, Kurt was lucky to remain on his feet as he was shoved down the hall. When they got closer to the door they'd just been talking about, Clint launched him toward it with a powerful boot to Kurt's ass.

The big man staggered forward, and after the kick, he fell with all of his weight against the door. Clint stayed put just long enough to watch as the door wasn't just knocked open, but taken clean off its hinges. All he could see in the room past that door was a wide desk and a few slender figures scrambling to see who the hell was making such an abrupt entrance.

"What is the meaning of this?" asked a man in a shrill voice. As Kurt tried to get back to his feet, the other men in that room parted like the Red Sea so another could get closer to the busted door. "What are you doing just standing there?" the shrill voice asked. "Do what I pay you to do!"

Keeping his hand on the grip of his Colt, Clint backed down the hall. It took several seconds for anyone inside that room to get a look out because Kurt was so large and so unsteady on his feet that he blocked them from seeing much past him. Moving past him was next to impossible. Clint waited until Kurt was finally able to step aside. When he saw the spindly, angry old man from the Tiger's Paw, Clint whispered, "I'll be damned. He wasn't lying to me after all."

The old man stood in the doorway and glared out as if he were angrily staring down the world and everyone in it. Clint wasn't the only one in the hall by now. There were half a dozen doors between the far end and the stairs, most of which were open so curious men and women in various states of undress could see what was happening.

Although his beady little eyes found Clint, the old man looked around at all the other faces staring back at him before shrieking, "Mind your own goddamn business! You," he said while stabbing a bony finger at Kurt, "get your ass in here and explain yourself. You are a disgrace!" His tirade continued, but was partially blocked out when one of the other men in that room propped the door back against its frame.

When it became clear that nobody was coming through that door for a while, Clint made his way to the stairs and started climbing down. His steps remained steady and purposeful as he kept his ears and eyes open for anything that might tell him someone was coming for him.

The customers on the second floor were amused but eager to get back to their rooms, and the girls watched Clint with beaming smiles.

As he continued down to the first floor, Clint was certain he would hear footsteps rushing to catch up to him or someone shouting for him to stop and answer for what had been done to Kurt. None of that came, however. There was a bit more noise inside Miss Tasha's than usual, but it seemed about right considering the commotion. The front door was in his sight when Clint finally got one of the confrontations he'd been expecting.

"Wait right there," Miss Tasha said as she stormed out of the back parlor. "I heard there was a fight, and you must be the cause of it. I can tell just by looking at you."

Clint brushed a hand against a spot marking one of the few lucky punches Kurt had managed to land while in his room upstairs. "You're right, ma'am."

"Get out," she snarled while pointing to the front door. "And don't come back."

"I was just on my way out," he replied, tipping his hat. "Good evening to you, Miss Tasha."

"Expect a bill from me when I get a look at the damage you caused."

Clint walked outside and found both Ingrid and the woman who'd escorted him upstairs waiting for him on the porch. Ingrid smiled and said, "Don't you pay a cent for no damages. Me and the girls will take up a collection."

"Much obliged," Clint said.

"I suppose I'll be coming to you to have that talk we mentioned earlier instead of you coming here."

"That'd be a good idea," he said.

Before Clint could take one more step, the redhead took his face in her hands and planted a kiss on his lips. "Cassidy," she said when she came up for air. "My name's Cassidy. I'll be coming as well."

"Now that sounds like a mighty good idea."

THIRTY-ONE

"Oh no!" Henrietta said as soon as she took a look at Clint's face. "They got to you again?"

Clint had barely made it through the front doors of the newly renamed Howling Hound Saloon before he was noticed. "Is Leo around?" he asked.

"Yes," she said from where she stood in the middle of a short row of tables being carried away. Two of the young men doing the carrying were Will and his brother. Upon seeing Clint, Will nodded once. Slapping the boy on the shoulder, Henrietta said, "Get back to what you were doing. That goes for all of you. And as for you," she said while approaching Clint, "get down here so I can get a better look at that mess you call a face."

"It's not as bad as it looks," Clint said as he stooped down so the short woman could put her hands on his cheeks.

"That's only because the last time you got your face messed up, it was a whole lot worse." Leaning back just a little, she asked, "Why are you smiling?"

"Because this time I gave a whole lot better than I got."

Henrietta smiled as well before letting go of Clint's

cheeks so he could stand fully upright again. "Well, at least that's something."

"What's going on here?" he asked while nodding at the short procession of tables headed toward the back of the room.

"We're opening a storeroom in the back and turning it into a parlor for faro and private card games," she told him. "In place of those tables up front, we're going to be getting a roulette wheel. Should be arriving on the stage later today or tomorrow."

Leo poked his head out from his office. He barely got a chance to nod to Clint before he was needed to oversee the placement of tables in the next room.

"How's he doing?" Clint asked.

Taking a quick glimpse toward the office, Henrietta was just in time to see Leo's back as he started issuing orders to the boys moving his furniture. "A little better. At least he's not moping so much. All things considered, I'd say it's a good improvement in a short stretch of time."

"Yeah, well, we don't have much time to work with. I'm going to have a word with him."

"Are you going to tell me what happened to your face or not?"

"Not," Clint said. Before she got too riled up, he added, "I'll tell Leo and he can tell you. When he does, I'm sure you'll understand why I'm in a hurry."

"I suppose that'll do for now." Fortunately for Clint's sake, she became distracted by an argument that sparked up between two gamblers at a poker game near the stage.

Madeline was up there practicing, and when a bottle was thrown by one of the gamblers, she quickly stepped down and rushed over to Clint. "Mr. Adams," she said while hurrying to catch up to him as he crossed the main room. "Mr. Adams, please can I just have a moment?"

Clint stopped at the bar and turned to her. "What's on your mind?" he asked.

"I want to thank you for what you're doing. I know the things Mr. Voss has been saying about me."

Clint had to think for a moment before he chuckled and said, "Oh, you mean Westin. It's difficult to think of him as a mister."

"Yes, well, he's a terrible man who looks at me like I'm a slab of beef on his plate. I shudder to think," she continued while actually shuddering, "what he would ever do to me if I took him up on his offer."

"Has he actually made the offer directly to you?"

"Yes. He told me I could come and work for him if I wanted to make more money. All I'd need to do is stop by his place over on Bale. Lord only knows what would happen if I ever went there."

"What place on Bale?" Clint asked.

"I think that's where he's staying. All I know for certain is that I can't go anywhere with him, and even if I held out for a while on my own, it would only be a matter of time before he tried something even bolder." Madeline's features may have been delicate, but she showed a strength deeper inside when she added, "If he can't get me, he'd just go after someone else. I can't allow that to happen."

"Well, neither can I," Clint assured her as he put his hands on her shoulders while looking her straight in the eyes. "Westin is already on the run. He just doesn't have anywhere to go yet. Before long, all you'll need to worry about is that pretty voice of yours."

Madeline smiled at that. "If there's anything you need me to do, just say so."

"All I need is for you to tell me exactly where Westin told you to go on Bale Avenue if you wanted to find him."

THIRTY-TWO

Clint walked into the storeroom as Will and his brother were coming out. Stepping aside so another young man could get past him, Clint looked around at a dusty room with cobwebs hanging from the rafters. It was twice as long as it was deep and had enough room to comfortably fit another two or three tables before becoming cramped.

"I didn't even know this room was back here," Clint said.

"Well, what the hell would you know?" Leo replied. "You barely been here for a week or so."

"Fair enough. How's the hand?"

"Lighter than it used to be."

Clint put his hands in his pockets. "So I guess you'll have to call for reinforcements if someone orders two fingers of whiskey?"

Leo wanted to be angry, but he just couldn't keep it up for long. Finally, he shook his head and muttered, "Damn it all to hell."

Clint walked up to him and gave him a pat on the back. "I know exactly what you mean. This isn't the sort of thing you expected you'd have to deal with when you decided to open your own saloon."

"Yeah, but what do I know? I thought the Dig Dog was a good name for the place."

"Maybe you should leave the bigger decisions to Henrietta."

"Not a bad idea."

"And neither is this," Clint said as he looked at the tables that were sloppily arranged on the unswept floor. "More gambling means a bigger house cut. And it seems you'll have something else to offer that'll make this place stand out."

"Please, Clint. Don't try to make me feel better. You've obviously got something to say, and it ain't about the new card room."

"You're right about that."

"And," Leo said in the silence that followed, "you're not too eager to tell me whatever it is you got to say."

"Right again."

"So just spit it out. My patience with pretty much everything has worn a bit thin."

Unable to come up with a better way to phrase it, Clint said, "Your problem with Westin may be bigger than we thought."

"We?"

"I told you before that I'm involved in this," Clint said.

Leo nodded before asking, "How much bigger?"

"I did some poking around and found one of Westin's men. The bald fellow. He was at Miss Tasha's."

"Not too surprising. She runs the cheapest whores in town."

"He was there for more than just the whores," Clint continued. "Miss Tasha is the one behind Westin for certain.

She's getting her place set up to take over as much of your business as she can after you're gone."

"That'd make her the one who wants to use my place for a warehouse for whatever contraband she wants to smuggle and as a front for the girls she wants to turn into slaves?"

"Partly. This is where things go from bad to worse."

Leo pulled in a deep breath and let it out with a huff. "Don't bother with the sweet talk," he said. "Just spit it out."

"Miss Tasha isn't working alone. In fact, I'm thinking she's actually working for someone else."

"Who?"

"An associate of Ki Dhang."

Leo's head hung forward like a puppet that had just gotten its string cut. "What the hell would Ki Dhang want with me? Or is this just another way for God to punish Leo Parker for some crime I committed in another life?"

"It may not be as bad as all of that."

"Ki Dhang is one of the richest men in New Mexico," Leo said. "He can snap his fingers and put a bullet into anyone he chooses. I mean, it was bad enough that my stepbrother had anyone at all backing his play. Now he's got Ki Dhang on his side?"

Leo paced the room. Every step he took brought another emotion to his weary face. "Why the hell didn't Ki just buy me out? That'd be a deal anyone could live with. Instead, he's got to go through all this trouble just to use me as a front for God knows what? That don't even make sense!"

"Exactly!" Clint said. "That doesn't make sense. I spoke with Ki Dhang for just a minute or two, and I could tell he doesn't do anything if it doesn't make sense. I've got a real good idea of what's going on, but I need to make certain, and once I do, this whole house of cards is going to fall."

Leo had been staring at the floor, taking in what he was

hearing. As he watched the barkeep slowly nod, Clint wondered what was going through his mind. If he wasn't willing to go any further, there wasn't a good reason for Clint to do more than see to Madeline's safety. If Leo was ready to see this through to the end, then that was a different story altogether. Clint didn't have to wait long to know which way the pendulum was swinging.

Looking up and wrapping his good hand around his bad one, Leo asked, "What do you want from me?"

"Things could get messy," Clint told him. "Messier than they've been so far. When your fingers were taken from you, that was meant as a taste of how bad things could get if—"

"I know what it was meant to tell me," Leo snapped. "I got that message real good. What I asked is what you want from me."

"I need you to keep an eye on Madeline just in case someone tries to take her the hard way. Be ready with that shotgun and keep your eyes open for the next day."

"Just one day?" Leo asked. "What happens after that?"

"One way or another, by that time this mess should be sorted out."

Leo didn't say anything after that. He didn't have to. The steely look in his eyes told Clint that he was in for the whole ride. Clint just had to make sure that ride didn't take them both to a shallow grave.

THIRTY-THREE

When Clint entered the Tiger's Paw this time, the entire place felt different than it had on his last visit. While there were fewer customers at the moment, the intensity at each table could be felt like a thick haze that stuck to his skin. Every breath he pulled into his lungs was tinged with exotic scents and flavors. Some of those came from the food that was being carried from the kitchen, but the rest drifted out from the pipes and cigars that were the stock-in-trade of any opium den.

The women who approached him weren't familiar. That didn't stop them from wrapping themselves around Clint's arms and rubbing his back while purring into his ear. "Welcome to Tiger's Paw," one of them said in a thick Chinese accent. The other woman spoke a different language to him, which wasn't nearly as interesting as the way she chewed on his earlobes between every other word.

"Where's Jade?" Clint asked.

"Not here," the first girl replied. "We take care of you just fine."

"I want to see Ki Dhang."

The second girl laughed while snaking her hand between his legs. "She thinks you want him instead of us," the first one explained. "I think you or Ki Dhang are not like that."

It wasn't easy to disentangle himself from the women, and many parts of him didn't want to succeed, but Clint managed to do so anyway. Holding the first one at arm's length, he said, "I'm not here for entertainment. I want to see Ki Dhang and I want to see him now. It's important."

When the second woman tried to press against him again, the first stopped her with a sharp stream of Chinese words. Shrugging, the second woman wandered off to find someone else to seduce.

"Mr. Dhang is very busy," the remaining woman said.

"Tell him Clint Adams wants to talk to him about someone who might be looking to stick a knife in his back."

"He does not like to be misled," she warned.

"I'm not misleading anyone. Just go and tell him."

"Very well. It's on your head."

Even though he wasn't about to give in to the advances of those women, that didn't stop Clint from enjoying the view as they walked away. Their dresses were so tight that they could very well have been painted onto their bodies, and both women knew exactly how to move within them. Less than a minute after the first woman had disappeared from sight, she returned to motion for Clint to meet her near the bar.

When he was close enough, she said, "Mr. Dhang will see you. This way."

She took him upstairs once again to the second floor. Ki Dhang sat at the same table where he'd been gambling the first time Clint had met him, but on this occasion he sat alone. There was a plate of noodles in front of him and a cup of hot tea in his hand.

"Minh says you have something important to tell me," Dhang said as Clint approached his table. "Something about a traitor among my men. Know that I do not take such threats lightly."

"I would think not," Clint replied. "Especially when it's someone who seems to be fairly close to you."

"And who would that be?"

"The old man who sat in that chair the last time I was here," Clint said while pointing to the spot where the angry man had been on his previous visit.

Ki Dhang scowled. "No matter what insults he may have hurled at you, that does not give you the right to make such an accusation."

"This doesn't have anything to do with the fit he threw when I came to see you last time. I've been insulted by much fouler mouths than his."

"He is Chow Sun. Does this name mean anything to you?"

"No."

"If you knew anything about the largest smuggling operation to cover Korea, China, and these United States, then you would not only know of Chow Sun but you would tremble at the mention of his name."

Clint couldn't imagine trembling after hearing any man's name. Telling Ki Dhang that, however, would have surely just put them at cross-purposes. Even though there was less than a handful of others sitting at different tables on that floor, Clint lowered his voice so their conversation wouldn't carry any farther than necessary. "With all due respect, I didn't come here just to throw around empty words."

Dhang nodded once. "Go on."

"I was over at Miss Tasha's to pay a visit to one of the men who I had a score to settle with. He and a man by the name of Westin Voss are trying to run the man who owns the Howling Hound out of Larga Noche."

Dhang shrugged as though he'd just been told about where a group of ants had decided to march next.

"This man I visited," Clint continued, "told me he was working on behalf of Miss Tasha herself. Turns out that she's got a partner as well and he's the important gentleman we were just discussing."

"Chow Sun?"

"That's right. He and Miss Tasha are working together to move some business of their own into town. Now if you already knew about this, then I apologize for stirring anything up without cause. Since none of them seemed too happy to be found out, I was guessing they were playing things close to the vest."

Pushing away his noodles and dabbing at his mouth with a linen napkin, Dhang squared his shoulders while studying Clint carefully. "What sort of business are they starting?" he asked.

"Smuggling, for a start. They also want to bring girls in through here before sending them who knows where."

"As slaves?"

"That was my understanding."

Dhang snarled a string of words under his breath. Even though Clint couldn't understand them, he could tell they weren't of the friendly variety. "I must make certain of this," he said while standing up and placing his hands upon the table.

"Can't say as I blame you."

"If you are lying, there will be consequences." Smiling politely, Dhang added, "But that does not mean you are to be treated as anything but my guest. You will be shown to one of my finest rooms, where you will wait in comfort for me to return."

"Why don't I just meet you back here?"

Dhang clapped his hands together once, which summoned a pair of burly gunmen to stand behind Clint on either side. "Go and await my return," Dhang said in a tone of voice that left no room for debate.

THIRTY-FOUR

Clint was shown into a room on that same floor, just down a short hallway with only two doors. That room was furnished with a couple of padded chairs, an expensive-looking washbasin centered upon an inlaid table, and a bed with a canopy that nearly reached the ceiling.

"If you are thirsty," the large man said as he pulled open a cabinet filled with liquor bottles.

"What if I feel like stretching my legs?" Clint asked. "Mind if I take a walk outside?"

"Mr. Dhang will only be a few hours."

"A few hours?"

"You will wait here."

"Now just hold on a second!" Clint said. Before he could finish, the man held out a thick paw of a hand.

"Your gun. Give to me, please."

"I'm not handing over my gun."

"Then I will take it from you."

Clint had sized up the man in front of him after a few seconds. Maybe the Colt could be taken from him by force and maybe Clint could keep that from happening. Either way, fighting with one of Ki Dhang's men wasn't exactly a good way to get on the big man's good side. Since he was already in this far, Clint eased the Colt from its holster and handed it over.

"Now let me look for anything else."

Since he'd come along this far, Clint raised his arms over his head.

"Wise choice," the burly escort said.

Clint let out a strained breath. "We'll see."

After searching Clint from heat to toe, Dhang's gunman found a knife in Clint's boot, which he took.

He then stepped out of the room and shut the door, leaving Clint to his own devices.

Although the room was quite comfortable, there wasn't much to keep him occupied for several minutes. The thought of sitting in there for hours made Clint fidget even more than he already was. When he heard the door opening again, he jumped up from where he'd been sitting and eagerly went to greet whoever was coming for him. "Oh," he grunted when he saw the same big fellow who'd taken away his Colt. "It's you again."

"You have visitors."

"Mr. Dhang's back already?"

"Not quite."

The thickly muscled guard stepped to one side, allowing two familiar but very unexpected guests to step into the room.

Stunned by what he was seeing, Clint said, "Ingrid? What the—"

The slender blonde cut him short by pressing her lips against his. Clint's eyes widened with surprise. Just behind her, Jade said a few words to the large fellow who'd brought them to that room before shutting the door in his face.

As soon as Ingrid pulled back a little, Clint picked up

right where he'd left off. "What the hell are you doing here?" he asked.

"Making sure you don't get killed," she whispered.

Clint didn't see Jade approach him so much as he felt when she was close enough to touch him. Her exotic scent drifted through the air as her fingernails raked gently against his back. "Mr. Dhang is having a word with Miss Tasha," she said. "This woman told him she is a friend of yours."

Ingrid's eyes were locked on Clint's as she rubbed against him. Slowly, Clint said, "Yes. She is. I just wasn't expecting to see her here."

"Since Mr. Dhang is conducting business with Miss Tasha, he agreed to let your friend come to help you pass the time," Jade said.

Clint turned and finally caught a glimpse of the dark-haired Asian woman. Jade was so close to him that all he could see was half of her face before she stepped behind him. "That's very generous of him," Clint said.

"Mr. Dhang treats his friends very well."

"So he considers me a friend?"

Jade's hands worked to expertly massage every muscle in Clint's back. "He is still deciding on that, but I am sure you have nothing to worry about. Until he makes his decision, I was told to keep you busy."

"And I insisted on coming along," Ingrid said in a sensual whisper. Her eyes, on the other hand, pleaded with Clint to go along with what she told him.

"I'm glad for that," he said. "Nobody can take my mind off things the way you can." Then, Clint wrapped his arms around Ingrid and kissed her deeply on the lips. She tasted sweet and melted against him while nibbling on his lower lip. While they continued to kiss, Jade walked toward the table near the bed, where she poured some water into a basin.

"Sometimes Dhang uses girls from Miss Tasha's to entertain his customers," Ingrid whispered directly into his ear. "Sometimes those customers don't make it out of here."

Clint looked over toward the bed and saw Jade was slowly peeling off her dress. Somehow knowing exactly when his eyes were on her, she looked over and smiled while dipping her fingers into the water she'd poured. Jade leaned her head back to rub some of the water along the slope of her neck.

"What's your plan?" Clint whispered.

"Right now," Ingrid replied while stroking his growing erection, "we need to bide our time."

"Sounds promising."

THIRTY-FIVE

Jade was stark naked as she approached Clint and began stripping him out of his clothes. More than just undressing him, she moved her hands along his body and over his pockets as though she was searching him for contraband. All things considered, he enjoyed that search a hell of a lot more than the one performed by the big guard. After removing his boots, Jade placed her hands on Clint's thighs and ran them all the way up as she rose to stand in front of him.

"Mr. Dhang takes good care of his friends," Jade said.

Clint cupped her pert breasts, paying special attention to her dark, penny-sized nipples. "How about we not talk about him for a while?"

"Good idea," she said while taking Clint's hand and guiding it between her legs. Jade's skin was smooth as silk, but the skin of her inner thighs felt more like warm cream. She closed her eyes and let out a slow breath as Clint's fingers found the little slit between her legs. The lips of her pussy were moist, and Clint rubbed them up and down until Jade grabbed on to his shoulder for support.

Suddenly, Clint felt a warm, wet sensation below his

waist. When he looked down, he saw Ingrid on her knees and licking the inside of his leg. With Jade standing slightly to Clint's side, Ingrid had to lean in from the other angle but she quickly wrapped her lips around his cock and began sucking him.

The longer Clint massaged Jade's pussy, the wetter she became. When he slipped a finger inside her, she gripped his shoulders tightly for support as she started moaning in her native tongue.

Ingrid was vigorously bobbing her head back and forth, devouring his cock while cupping him in one hand. She only came up for air once, and then she ran her tongue up and down his rigid shaft.

Before long, Jade stepped away from him and set herself down on the bed. Sitting on the edge of the mattress with her legs hanging over, she lay back and used both hands to spread her pussy lips apart. Clint may not have known the exact words she was saying, but he could recognize the pleading tone in her voice. After helping Ingrid to her feet, Clint approached the bed. Jade watched them both with hungry eyes, rubbing herself as Clint drew closer. She then propped herself up on one elbow, reached out, and guided Clint's stiff cock to where she so desperately wanted it to go.

Clint took hold of Jade's legs and drove into her. Both he and Jade let out satisfied moans, and when Clint buried himself just a bit deeper into her, Jade gripped the expensive blankets with both hands and arched her back. As Clint fell into a steady thrusting movement, Jade wrapped one leg tightly around his waist while allowing him to open the other leg just a bit wider.

As this was going on, Ingrid kept busy as well. Clint felt her press against his back and then start to gently run her fingernails up and down his body. Next, he felt her hair brush against the side of his face as well as the wet touch of her mouth against his ear.

"If she gets the signal from Dhang's men," Ingrid whispered, "she'll kill you."

Clint felt a rush of anxiety when he heard Ingrid's voice. However, the blonde's whisper was nowhere near loud enough to be heard above the creak of the bed and Jade's steady grunting as Clint pumped into her. In between his own breaths, Clint half grunted and half whispered, "Signal?"

Wrapping her arms around him from behind so she could rub his bare chest, Ingrid said, "Don't know exactly, but if she gets it, you won't leave this room alive and neither will I."

Clint looked back just far enough to kiss Ingrid on the lips. He continued pumping between Jade's legs as he whispered, "I'm unarmed."

"Don't worry about that. Just be ready."

"You, too."

"I'm always ready," Ingrid said. She then rested her chin on Clint's shoulder and said, "I feel left out."

Opening her eyes as if she'd just awoken from a deep sleep, Jade replied, "We can't have that, now can we?" She wriggled away from Clint so she could flip over and crawl toward the opposite end on all fours.

While Clint was captivated by that sight, hc was roughly turned around and shoved toward the bed until he dropped down onto the mattress in a seated position. "You're a real silver-tongued devil," Ingrid said. "Put that tongue to work on me." Even though she wasn't stripped bare like the other two, Ingrid was still a sight to behold. She tugged at the strings fastening the front of her loose blouse, which allowed the thin material to fall aside to reveal her nicely rounded breasts. Large, pink nipples were already erect as she gathered up her plain brown skirt to hike it up past her knees.

As Ingrid climbed onto the bed and straddled Clint's chest, Jade busied herself with the lower portion of his body. Clint couldn't see what she was doing, but he could feel her tongue flick against his erection as well as her delicate hand wrap around his cock.

Ingrid scooted forward while reaching down to grab Clint's hair in one hand. With the other hand, she pulled up her skirt a bit more to show him the Derringers that were strapped so high up her inner thighs that they would have easily been overlooked during a simple search. Once she was certain that Clint had seen the guns, she placed herself even higher up on his chest while pulling his head between her legs.

Clint was all too happy to oblige her by licking the smooth lips of Ingrid's pussy. When his tongue found the sensitive nub of her clit, she leaned back and let out a shuddering moan.

While this was going on, Jade straddled Clint's hips and took him inside her. He could feel her legs squeezing in on him from both sides as she rode him with growing intensity. She took every inch of him inside and moaned loudly as Clint started to pump up into her. Eventually, she found a spot she liked and stayed there while slowly grinding on him.

At first, Ingrid had moaned loudly even when she'd lifted herself up a bit to put about an inch of space between herself and Clint's mouth. He looked up at her, cupped her ass in his hands, and stuck his tongue inside her to drive Ingrid out of her mind with surges of pleasure. Soon, she lost herself in the moment and trembled like a leaf as she felt an orgasm sweep through her entire body.

When Clint looked up, he could see slender hands

cupping Ingrid's breasts from behind. Jade teased the other woman's nipples between her thumb and forefinger, grunting louder and louder as Clint continued to thrust between her legs. It wasn't long before Jade was screaming with ecstasy and tossing her hair back and forth.

Between watching Ingrid, tasting her, feeling Jade, and hearing them both cry out in pleasure, Clint couldn't hold himself back another second. He pumped up inside Jade and exploded within her with a climax that seemed to last the better part of a day. As the girls' cries faded and the blood rushed a little slower through Clint's ears, another sound could be heard.

Knocking.

All three of them quieted down and Ingrid climbed off Clint to sit beside him on the bed. Jade remained sitting astride him, sweat trickling down her taut body, and turned toward the door. After she said something in her native language, a gruff voice replied through the door. There was one more quick exchange before Jade turned to look down at Clint.

He didn't need a translator to know that a signal had just been given.

THIRTY-SIX

Still straddling Clint's hips, Jade reached up into her thick black hair. She arched her back, displaying her proud breasts as she removed a thin polished stick that had been keeping a portion of her hair in place. With the snap of her wrist, she pulled the stick apart to reveal a short stiletto blade that had been hidden within the stick. Before Clint could make a move, she pressed the tip of the blade against a tender spot on Clint's inner thigh.

"What's this about?" Clint asked.

"You have become a liability to Mr. Dhang," Jade said.

"And that's why you're going to stick me in the leg?"

"I am sorry, but that is why I must kill you."

"Better men have tried with much heavier artillery than that," Clint replied.

Jade smiled while slowly twisting the tip of the stiletto against Clint's leg. "All I need to do is open this artery and you will bleed out faster than if you were shot."

"That's a hell of a way to treat a man while you're still sitting on top of him."

"Is it not the best way to die while the pleasures I have given you are still fresh?"

Clint had to admit that would be a damn fine way to go, but he wasn't about to say that to her. "You could always let me go," he offered.

She shook her head. Now that the stick had been removed from her hair, Jade's long black mane hung loose to make her look even more like a jungle cat. "The order has been given and there is nothing for me to do about it. At least the two of you will leave this world with the taste of life's greatest pleasures fresh on your—"

Ingrid pounced at her with both arms stretched out, catching both Jade and Clint by surprise. Jade fell straight back, pinning Clint's legs to the bed. Although he was trapped in an awkward position, he was grateful that the sharp, slender blade had been forced well away from his leg and the other vital spots in that general vicinity.

"Too much talking," Ingrid said as she delivered a right cross to Jade's head.

Even though Jade took the punch well for someone her size, she was knocked completely off the bed and hit the floor in a tangle of smooth legs, long hair, and scrambling arms. Somehow she managed to right herself and snap a quick punch to answer the one she'd been given. Having caught Ingrid before she could take another swing at her, Jade got to her feet and shouted something at the door.

"Clint!" Ingrid said.

In the flurry of commotion that had descended upon that bed, he'd rolled off the side and landed on his feet. When he heard Ingrid call his name, he stood up straight and caught the pistol she'd tossed his way. The little Derringer was swallowed up in his hand, but his finger found the trigger quickly enough.

When the door was shoved open, Clint waited just long enough to get a look at who was coming in. It was no surprise to see the burly guard come stomping in like a bull. Not only was he holding a .44, but he brought the pistol up and took aim at Clint. The instant he saw that, Clint fired from the hip. The Derringer popped once, causing the big man to flinch. Clint took more careful aim and squeezed off his second shot a split second before the other man could fire. That bullet caught the guard in the forehead and snapped his entire upper body back. Another shot cracked through the air, and when Clint turned to see what had happened, he found Ingrid holding the second Derringer in her grip.

"She . . . was going to kill me," Ingrid gasped.

Jade lay crumpled on the floor. She let out a groan, rolled onto her back, and showed the bloody wound in her ribs.

"She'll make it," Clint said as he walked over to take the pistol away from the dead man in the doorway. On his way back into the room, he kicked the stiletto away from Jade's hand. "Let me know if anyone else comes along."

Ingrid was stunned, but she nodded and watched the door while Clint pulled on his pants, shirt, and boots. When he was dressed, he asked, "Is there any law around here?"

"There's a county sheriff in the next town."

"That'd be a no. Can you keep an eye on her for a short while?"

Ingrid nodded. "I'll tie her up before she gets any ideas."

Since Jade was still sluggish after receiving the shallow bullet wound, Clint figured she wouldn't be much of a threat anytime soon. "If she gets a second wind," he told her, "don't hesitate to put her down."

He'd said that mostly for Jade's benefit and she cringed in response to the threat. Although Ingrid seemed nervous, she gained some confidence when Clint went back to the guard, searched him, and then tossed her the holdout pistol he found in the bigger man's boot.

"When you hear things quiet down, get the hell out of here," he said.

"What about you?"

"I'm going to make a bit more noise."

THIRTY-SEVEN

If there was one advantage to gunfire, it was how quickly it could clear a room. As Clint headed for the stairs, he crossed paths with only one armed man on the second floor. All the gamblers were either gone or hiding under tables. That single gunman wasn't expecting to see anyone storm down the hallway, and he dropped to the floor when Clint fired a warning shot into the ceiling over the man's head.

Clint ran down the stairs, holding the dead guard's .44 in plain sight as a warning to anyone who might get in his way. Although there were more armed men on the main floor, none of them tried to get in his way. Upon reaching the door that led to the street, Clint meant to ask where he could find Ki Dhang. He got a good idea of where he needed to go when he heard gunshots from the other side of Sharp Bend.

Women screamed from inside the cathouse. Something cast a large shadow on the front window before the glass shattered from the impact of something large being tossed outside. Clint tensed while sighting along the top of his barrel. The man who'd been thrown outside was wrapped partially in the curtains that had been yanked from the windows and were slowly pulled aside by a bloody hand.

"Hello there, Kurt," Clint said while smiling down at the battered bald man cocooned inside thick layers of purple velvet. "This just ain't your day."

"Adams! Thank God!" Kurt scrambled to free himself from the curtain and climb to his feet. When he saw Clint point the .44 at him, he quickly tossed away the gun that he'd almost forgot he'd been holding. "Them Chinese are out of their damn minds!"

"What's going on in there?" Clint asked.

"They're about to kill each other!" Kurt had plenty more he wanted to say, but was silenced by an eruption of gunfire coming from the first floor of Miss Tasha's. Even Clint had to flinch as several pistol shots cracked amid the thunderous roar of a shotgun firing both its barrels in quick succession.

Having reflexively dropped to one knee, Clint waited until the shots faded before standing up again. When he saw Kurt looking to him for instruction, Clint told him the first thing that came to mind. "Run. If I see you again, I'll shoot you on sight."

"Fair enough," Kurt said before racing down the street like a horse bolting from a burning stable.

Clint approached Miss Tasha's, scooping up the pistol Kurt had dropped along the way. Since the window had neither glass nor curtains in it, he could see straight through to the front room. Every piece of furniture was overturned. Several men lay on the floor, crumpled and bloodied by whatever hell had been unleashed in that place. Striding down the stairs as if he were taking a stroll through a park, Ki Dhang made his way to the front door. He looked at the carnage, but seemed more puzzled by the shattered window and the fact that Clint was standing on the other side of it.

"Son of a bitch!" shrieked a voice from within the

building. Screaming a string of obscenities in at least two different languages, Chow Sun stomped down the stairs carrying a pistol that seemed heavier than his entire body. "You die, bastard!"

Ki Dhang's expression hardly changed as he turned to get a look behind him. Even when he caught sight of the crazy old man coming down the stairs, he didn't make a move to defend himself.

Clint acted out of reflex. Bringing up the .44 he'd taken, he fired a shot that caught the old man in the chest and sent him tumbling the rest of the way down the staircase.

Another pair of armed men rushed into the front room from the direction of the parlor. Clint snapped his aim toward them to defend himself, but Dhang stopped those men in their tracks with a swiftly raised hand and a few clipped words. Looking to Clint, Dhang said, "You are a wise man, Mr. Adams. I appreciate your choice of targets."

"I never did like that guy," Clint said. "Now there's still the matter of you sending that woman to kill me."

"Jade is but one of the traitors on my payroll whose head was turned by the lure of Chow Sun's money. Since you still live, I trust you have dealt with her?"

"She's alive."

"Then I shall deal with her. I owe you a great debt," Dhang said. "Chow was poised to do much damage to me and my business by dirtying my name with his filthy slavery. What happened here will not go unpunished. If there is something you require of me, you merely need to ask."

"I'll get back to you on that."

Clint went back to the Howling Hound to check on Leo. Before he even got through the front door, Leo rushed outside shouting, "She's gone! They took her!"

"Who's gone?" Clint asked. "Madeline?"

"No! Henrietta. Westin came by when all the shooting started down the street and grabbed her. I don't know where they went."

"I believe I do."

THIRTY-EIGHT

Clint had become an expert at navigating Larga Noche's twisting streets. He made it to Bale Avenue in no time at all thanks to cutting across several alleys and a few back lots. Following the simple directions Madeline had given to him, Clint found the little house that was supposedly being used by Westin Voss. When he saw Westin lean out a window to take a shot at him, Clint knew he'd found the right place.

The shot was hurried and sailed well above its mark. Clint ran in a crooked line to avoid catching any other wild shots and kicked in the house's front door as soon as he was close enough. Standing inside a modestly furnished room, Westin had his pistol in one hand and his other hand hanging on to the collar of Henrietta's dress.

"What are you doing, Westin?" Clint asked.

Westin's eyes were wild, and when they darted to a nearby door, he wailed, "No!"

The door creaked open just enough for Clint to see Samuel's face and the barrel of a shotgun. Without hesitation, Clint pulled the second gun he'd collected with his left hand and fired several shots through the door in a tight grouping.

The one-armed man fell forward and dropped face-first into a heap.

"I've had enough of you," Clint said. "Let the woman go."

Petrified by how easily his partner had been sent to hell, Westin grabbed Henrietta's collar and pulled her close. She barely came up to his chin, but he hid behind her as if she were a brick wall. "The old man," Westin sputtered. "He promised we'd all be rich."

"Chow's dead," Clint told him. "And so is anyone else associated with him. Because you're Leo's brother, I'll give you a chance to get out of town before Dhang comes looking for you."

"Miss Tasha was in on it, too."

"And I'm sure Dhang has plans for her."

"I can't . . . I won't . . ." The more Westin tried to speak, the fewer words he could get out.

As Westin's gun drifted closer to Henrietta's temple, Clint growled, "Let her go, damn it!"

But Westin was too far gone. His eyes took on a crazy spark, prompting Clint to fire a shot that whipped over Henrietta's head and drilled through Westin's shoulder. When Westin hit the floor, Clint pulled Henrietta away and kicked his gun aside. "Next time you hide behind a prisoner," he said to the wounded outlaw, "find someone taller."

THIRTY-NINE

"Thank you, thank you, a thousand times thank you!" Leo said as he vigorously shook Clint's hand the following day.

"I think you've already thanked me a thousand times, but you're welcome all the same."

"I appreciate you not killing Westin, even though he deserved it. Next time the county sheriff comes through town, he'll be taking Westin along with him." Leo's face brightened when he added, "The good part is that after all that gun smoke cleared, Ki Dhang came by to make me a partner! He's headed out to California and he's letting me take over the Tiger's Paw! I can make any changes I like!"

"That's great, Leo."

"Since Miss Tasha's nowhere to be found, her girls are working for me as well. Suddenly, I own three places instead of just one!"

"Just try not to name any of them after dogs," Clint said as he tipped his hat to the excited barkeep.

Henrietta and Madeline were both waiting for Clint as he made his way to the door. The young singer gave him a hug along with a kiss on the cheek before getting back to the stage.

"Are you sure you can't stay?" Henrietta asked. "We could use you."

"I think I'll decline. The saloon business is too difficult a trade for a man like me."

Watch for

LET IT BLEED

397th novel in the exciting GUNSMITH series
from Jove

Coming in January!